Shlomo Kalo / THE TROUSESRS
Parables for the 21st Century

I0691474

English translation by Philip Simpson

© All Rights Reserved
Y   D.A.T. Publications
POBox 27019, Jaffa 61270, Israel
Fax: +972-3-5070458
Email: dat@y-dat.co.il
www.y-dat.com

ISBN: 978-965-7028-66-7
3rd edition with Amazon CreateSpace 2016

Cover Painting by Michel Delacroix

Shlomo Kalo

The Trousers

Parables
for the 21st Century

Y D.A.T. Publications

Table of Contents

The Trousers

The inhabitants of a large industrial town, some of whom were exceedingly wealthy while others merely aspired to be so, found themselves in a strange, complex and embarrassing predicament, the like of which they had never experienced before, and from which there seemed to be no escape: every year, with the coming of spring, the bodies of all the inhabitants of the town – young and old, babies, women and men, without exception – became covered with pink sores, the size of walnuts and just as hard. The sores were unbearably painful all through the spring, disappearing in summer only to reappear the following year, with the coming of a new spring. The local doctors, renowned for their skills throughout the land and even beyond its borders, were helpless; nor could their colleagues from neighbouring lands do anything to help.

With the utter failure of medical science – wisdom, knowledge and commonsense proving utterly powerless – all the worthies of the town and its most respected citizens convened an urgent meeting. After prolonged and wearisome debate, the decision was taken to appeal to the Almighty; perhaps He in His mercy would be disposed to bring healing, where the brilliant intellect and the much-vaunted resourcefulness of His creatures had achieved nothing.

So all the residents of the town put forward their pleas before God Almighty, and they entreated Him most earnestly, calling upon Him to see their suffering and ease their pain, and have compassion upon them and upon their wives and their old folk and the infants at their feet, and send to them a wise and understanding messenger, a miraculous counsellor, to deliver them from this terrible scourge that had befallen them for all the evil that they had done, and put an end to their suffering. So that days of light and joy would finally return, and their happiness never again be taken from them.

And God heard, and He sent to the tormented residents of the town, so helpless and forlorn, an angel in the form of a man to ease their suffering and heal their affliction, as they had beseeched Him.

And the messenger of the Lord descended from the heavens to the busy streets of the town. He mounted a raised platform in one of the squares, and appealed to the passers-by. He called out to them in a loud voice:

"Your prayers have been heeded, and your pleas have fallen on attentive ears! The Lord, merciful and gracious, long-suffering and ever kind, has heard your prayers, and at His command I have been sent to you to deliver you from the torment that surrounds you and from the catastrophe that has befallen you. Come to me and be healed of your affliction, and be delivered from your agony, and never again know misery and misfortune!"

And the messenger of the Lord, standing on the platform in the heart of the bustling town, fell silent and waited for the afflicted, desperate citizens to come to him for healing. And he stood waiting from morning until evening, and from evening until morning, and no one approached him, not even to bid him good day.

And the messenger descended from the platform and mingled with the suffering populace. He approached one man and asked him:

"Are you not the ones who beseeched the Lord Almighty, humbly imploring Him to send His angel to cure you of your pain? You see – He has heard your prayers and sent me to you to bring you healing and put an end to your torment... So why do you not come to be cured?"

And the other said to him in reply:

"We do not believe that you are the man of God or His sacred messenger, and that is why no one will approach you to consult you or hear what you have to say, not even bid you good day!"

"Why do you not believe that I have been sent by God the Most High, and why do you not approach me even to bid me good day?" – inquired the messenger, uncomprehending.

"Clear and distinct signs testify to the fact that you have not come from the presence of the Lord, nor have you been sent by the Blessed One!" – was the citizen's angry response.

"And what are these clear and distinct signs?" the messenger queried, and the other replied in a decisive tone that would brook no argument:

"It is the trousers that you wear!" He hastened to explain his meaning: "Is it possible that a messenger of the Lord, one whose wisdom is greater than that of any human being, who is mightier than any warrior of the past, the present or the future – would wear such shabby trousers, hanging so loosely and shapelessly on the body, as those trousers of yours? They do not conform to the dictates of fashion and they arouse derision and scorn in the minds of all who see them. Was it a pauper that sent you?" And the citizen concluded his speech in the same aggressive tone: "It is our firm and unanimous opinion that you are not the messenger of the Lord, nor are you His faithful servant; you are nothing but a miserable impostor, a beggar!" He turned away with an ostentatious air of contempt, and went about his business, disappearing from view.

The messenger of the Lord was baffled by the townspeople and their way of thinking, and dumbfounded by their obstinacy. He appealed to the One who had sent him, and asked to have his clothing changed, to have those shabby, shapeless and undignified trousers turned into new ones, the kind that the townspeople wore and considered fashionable. And before his request was even completed, his clothing was changed: his trousers were brand-new, elegant and stylish, immaculately tailored in accordance with the very latest fashion – the best quality available in that place and at that time.

And the messenger of God returned to the streets and the marketplaces, the bustling squares and boulevards of that town, and he called out again:

"Come to me all those of you who implored God the Most High to send you His angel, to heal you of your afflictions and erase sorrow and pain from your hearts, and bring you salvation. You will suffer no more, and joy will return to your dwellings, and your spirits will be glad! Come, and delay no longer," the messenger cried, adding: "I am the one that you hoped and prayed for, an envoy of God who brings you solace in His name. I am he!"

And he climbed stairs and entered one of the public halls of the town, used for assemblies and civic gatherings, and waited for the people to come to him for healing. And he waited in vain, for no one approached, and no one came near. His very existence was ignored.

Utterly baffled and confused the messenger left the hall and again appealed to one of the passers-by, asking him the same question as before: why was no one coming to him for healing, although this was the purpose for which he had been sent.

The man looked at the messenger with loathing, as if shocked by his effrontery – daring to accost him with such a question. He declared:

"It is because of the trousers that you wear!" And he went on to explain: "Are we to believe that Almighty God, the creator and controller of all the worlds, would send down His angel dressed in elegant trousers conforming to the latest earthly style, fit only for hedonists, for mindless and frivolous mortals? Whatever became of humility, of reverence, of dignified simplicity and enlightened self-effacement? Only a scoundrel, or a charlatan, would wear such pretentious attire!" And he concluded forcefully: "We shall not come near you, nor shall we listen to what you have to say. We are not going to fall into the cunning and malicious trap that you have set for us!"

Hearing this diatribe, the messenger of the Lord fell silent, and for some time he stood motionless, as if turned to stone, while a crowd of curious onlookers began to gather around him. Suddenly the angel fell to his knees, and raising his face and arms heavenwards, he called upon his Father who had sent him, crying out to Him in anguish:

"My holy Father, they do not want you!"

At that moment the divine messenger disappeared from the sight of the curious, who had been staring at him with condescension and undisguised contempt. And the crowd was struck with awe and puzzlement, and there were those who said:

"This was indeed the angel that we hoped for, who came to bring solace to our souls and cure us of our afflictions, and put an end to our torment!"

But as the chronicles of the town reveal, those who held this opinion were soon shouted down by the majority, by those who noisily insisted on their version of events:

"Nonsense! He was nothing but an impostor and a conjuror! Would an angel of God wear such trousers?"

The townspeople were not delivered and their affliction, instead of subsiding and disappearing, became fiercer still and no longer abated with the coming of summer, but continued throughout the year, persisting even in the autumn and the winter. And the town was shrouded in deep mourning and beset by anguish and unspeakable pain. And the people stopped appealing to God; they maintained that He was not listening to them and was not concerned for their welfare, and in fact – He might just as well not exist.

The Man and the Tiger

A man is being pursued relentlessly by a bloodthirsty tiger. He reckons he has no chance of escaping his deadly pursuer; he cannot save himself. However strong his desire to evade the fearful clutches of the tiger, it is beyond his strength. Until in his bitter despair he decides to put an end to the chase in the only way possible – by leaping into the abyss; anything rather than fall victim to the tiger's claws. He runs like a maniac and stops on the edge of the cliff, tensed for the fateful jump. He is on the point of leaping from the jagged promontory, when on the rocky floor of the abyss he catches sight of a dozen hungry tigers, poised to rip him apart even before his skull is smashed on the stone. The quarry has no choice but to revise his original plan: at the very last moment he plucks up his courage and turns, seething with the fury that follows despair, resolved to confront the tiger, come what may. The tiger lunges at him with a murderous pounce... whereupon the apparently doomed man breaks into peals of laughter, for he sees this is not the lethal tiger that has been pursuing him down the ages but only – a cat. The cat leaps at him, panic-stricken, before making his escape with a plaintive wail.

The Wondrous Princess

Long, long ago, in the age of miracles, there lived a princess, whose beauty was as the rising dawn, whose wisdom was divine, the light of whose spirit shone throughout the land. Anyone who chanced to linger in her presence, if only for a short while, went on his way emboldened and rejoicing, his heart aglow with limpid light, with purity the like of which he had never known. This princess had striven with death and had prevailed, thus becoming immortal, and whosoever should take her to wife – to him too the gift of immortality was promised, in addition to all the other virtues with which his lady was blessed.

No wonder then, that in all the royal households existing in those times throughout the world, there was talk of the wondrous princess, and all the world's princes took a keen interest in her. Among them, five hundred were not content with this, but leaving behind them their sumptuous palaces and their glittering regalia, they came to the household of the princess and paid court to her assiduously, by day and by night, swearing to her solemn vows, declaring to her, severally and in chorus, that life without her would be no life, and death was to be preferred to expulsion from her royal portals, whatever the circumstances. They did not mean to budge from her household until she had chosen from among them all the one most worthy of her.

She decided to accede to their request, and to choose the one most worthy of her, and she set a test for them.

The princess declared that in one week's time she would stand on the bank of a deep and broad river, and whosoever should swim across the river and be the first to reach her – him she would marry and his wife she would be.

Off ran the princes with all haste to the rivers near and far – preparing, exercising, rehearsing their river-crossings, and resorting to abstinence and prayer, and on the appointed day – no signal was needed – they all came running and leaping like a storm-wind, frantically almost, leaving behind the world and all that was in it; no sight before their eyes other than the glorious image of the princess, their noble aspiration, their heart's one desire.

And when they arrived at the bank of the river that they must cross, on the other side of which stood the princess, waiting for the worthiest of them all to come and win her – they were greeted by a most unpleasant surprise: the whole of the broad river teemed with crocodiles hungry for flesh and with all kinds of murderous and venomous monsters from days of old, their cold eyes glinting with menace, freezing the hearts of all who saw them.

The eager princes' headlong rush braked, then

came to a stop altogether. There was no need for reconsideration of the facts which were only too evident in the sight of all, no pause for logical and scholarly reflection. There and then, the princes decided that they preferred their mortal lives above certain death in the quest for immortality; better to return to their homes, to comforts and excesses and indulgences of all kinds, than qualify, before their time, for a heart-rending royal requiem.

Of course, as in any fable worthy of the name, there was one man found who was utterly unlike the rest. He did not restrain his prancing feet, did not slacken his pace, did not hesitate to the slightest degree, did not ponder or analyse the facts that were so clearly visible to all; his firm resolution, that life without the fantastic princess was no life – was unshaken. In the grip of that holy madness, the madness of those who are created without fear – he leapt into the water, into the midst of the crocodiles and monsters.

And greatly to his surprise – not one monster pounced upon him, nor chased him nor tried to fasten its teeth around his throat or snatch him up alive. Suddenly he understood: all these creatures were nothing but hides – the stuffed skins of monsters and crocodiles.

So the stout-hearted, fearless prince crossed over the river and fell into the outstretched arms of his princess, his heart's desire. He won her, for there was none more worthy of her than he.

The Apple Tree

Once there was an apple tree, growing proudly among the trees of the forest. A fine tree which, in the season of apples, bore fruit of the finest quality, and before the other trees of the forest had occasion to begin whispering among themselves, he declared clearly and unequivocally – that all belonged to all, and would be offered to all, willingly and joyfully.

"By all means," he cried, "anyone who needs an apple, may he be so good as to draw near, take, eat his fill with pleasure and bless his creator for His grace, before continuing on his way refreshed and in good heart!"

The trees of the forest saw that among them there had arisen a tree that was not only of prodigious height, like those trees of ancient times, but was also endowed with generosity of spirit and of heart to match his stature; the trees of the forest delighted in him, admired him and revered him and were proud of him, and when a weary traveller happened along, they were eager to direct him towards the handsome tree – to enjoy the sight thereof, to take of the ripe fruit and bless its delicate fragrance and its fine taste, before going on his way with renewed vigour.

The wayfarer approached the tree and held out his hand – to the finest and the biggest apple. The tree hastened to admonish him in soft and polite language:

"Why that one? Take something more modest – as befits your status!"

The wayfarer was ashamed of himself, changed his mind and made to pick an apple of medium size.

But the watchful tree responded once again:

"Leave that for the one whom comes after you. You – be content with something less... Thus you will learn humility and self-denial!"

The flustered wayfarer hastily picked the first apple that came to hand, a tiny fruit that was barely ripe, and went on his way.

After the first wayfarer came a second, and the episode was repeated, with one small variation; the tree excused his behaviour with the assertion that the biggest apple was reserved for the purpose of supporting its offspring, meaning the seeds within, which, on falling to the ground, would need its flesh for a mulch, to ensure healthy growth for the future, to the delight of man and beast.

In the wake of the second came the third – and the story was the same, not changing even with the fourth and the fifth. Into the hearts of the trees of the forest doubt began to creep, and quickly this doubt turned to bitterness and disappointment. In place of the former joy and reverence and admiration, came confusion, shame and resentment. The trees of the forest stared down at the ground, not even wanting to look at their friend of former times, the arrogant apple tree – so generous with promises and so adept at avoiding fulfilment. The atmosphere was heavy, unbearable at times. But this was not to last for long.

One sultry day, from the thickets of the forest a motley gang of robbers emerged, and paying no heed whatsoever to the erudite speech and eloquent delivery of the apple tree, his gentle and courteous style – they fell upon him, stripped off all of the fruit, complete with the leaves and the twigs, broke and uprooted to their heart's content, and finally disappeared as suddenly as they had come, leaving the tree naked, bereft of fruit and foliage alike, in pain and distress, weeping and pleading for help.

Someone nevertheless took pity on him and he did not expire, but remained in his ugly and denuded state, groaning for himself, his pleasant mode of speech gone for ever; all that was left for him was to take thorough stock, and weep bitterly for the errors of his youth. Had he known then the proper way to behave – he would have assured himself of that coveted joy in which there is no disappointment, which is the lot of the one who promises and keeps his promises, whose heart is kind and whose spirit generous, whose hand is ever outstretched to give.

To Fly in the Air

High in the Himalayan mountains, on one of the steepest peaks, a Tao master, advanced in years, chose to make his abode. He had few pupils and fewer visitors – since life on the mountain was not easy, nor was access to it. In spite of this, his name was known far and wide, and all kinds of myths and legends were woven around his personality and his miraculous qualities. People said, access to the mountain was dangerous and circuitous because the old man himself had cast a spell on the place; it was also said that he could fly in the air and make himself seeing but unseen. These stories took wing, naturally enough, and were it not for the hazards of the steep and narrow path, the only way of reaching his cave, perched on the edge of the abyss – the curious would have flocked thither in their hordes.

Five pupils shared the capacious cave with him – the cave which opened on one of the most delightful corners of the mountain. Around it a splendid vegetable garden was cultivated, and fruit trees blossomed in the spring. In winter, white clouds scudded at the feet of the seekers after truth, and a sea of grey mist stretched from one horizon to another. In summer, the teacher and his pupils used to spend the night outside the cave, stretched out on the soft and dense carpet of grass, and calmly regarding the deep velvet sky, encrusted with great stars. In the autumn, the pupils and the teacher had work to do, preparing supplies of food for the winter and checking that their home was proof against the weather. And all the year round the pupils were constantly engaged in meditation, under the strict guidance of their teacher.

One after the other the years passed, and the long and sparse beard of the sage was enriched with fine silver threads, but as yet not a single one of his pupils had succeeded in breaking through the barrier of illusion and earning the grace of true freedom. Awareness of this fact grieved the pupils, and some asked themselves what was to become of them, when the time came for their teacher to take leave of his temporal body and be united fully with the one reality, that is ever constant. Who would then be their teacher?

One bright summer day, in the early afternoon, the pupils saw a traveller approaching, hurriedly climbing the steep and narrow path that skirted the abyss. When the sun kissed the horizon line and set the whole length of it ablaze, the man appeared before them, panting like a steam engine, flushed of face and yet – with a look of limpid clarity in his smiling eyes.

After exchange of courteous greetings and the offer of a cup of water, the guest was asked the routine question:

"What brings you here?"

"I want to know the truth!" he replied with vehemence.

"The truth is not something that is known," the pupil retorted, and another added:

"The man who seeks to know the truth, shows that he is unworthy of it."

The guest, a man in his early thirties, was unabashed:

"I don't know if the truth is known or not, and if I am worthy of it," he declared, adding in a firm tone: "But as to you – how can you be so sure of what you say?"

The pupils looked down and were silent. A long time passed and no one said a word. And then suddenly, in the entrance to the cave, appeared the figure of the elderly sage. The guest stepped forward at once, then fell prostrate at his feet and announced solemnly:

"I will not rise from this position until you promise to accept me as your pupil and teach me the ways of truth!"

The onlookers exchanged surprised glances. It was clear to all of them that the young man lying prone in the dust at the teacher's feet, hands outstretched and face to the ground, voice clear and firm – would assuredly fulfil his threat; he would not stand up, until the end of all generations, if the sage refused to grant his request.

After a while, the sage declared, in a voice made

hoarse by the weight of the years, and by the silence in which he had been immersed for many days:

"From this moment on you are my pupil in all things and it is your duty to obey me in all things – now rise and stand before me!"

"And will you guide me to the truth?" – the young man persisted.

"To the place where I am capable of guiding you, there I shall guide you!" – came the answer.

The new pupil rose from the ground, shook the dust from his clothes and stood in tense anticipation. His eyes shone with unfathomable happiness.

The sage took his seat among his pupils and signalled to the new pupil to join them. A young evening deepened the silence, and when the first stars rose in the heights of the limpid firmament, the old sage turned to the guest and said:

"All that I can teach you, is to fly in the air and to be seeing and unseen. If this is to your taste – you are welcome to stay, and if not – then go back the way that you came!" And so saying he rose from his seat, turned towards the cave and disappeared inside it.

Surprised and disappointed, the resolute young man looked into the blank faces of the five seekers after truth:

"Was it for this that I made my way from faraway Nanking to this godforsaken desert?" – he complained, his words directed more towards himself than towards the others. "People were right then," he added, pouring out the bitterness of his heart – "when they said he was nothing but a magician, and not one of the greatest teachers, as I mistakenly thought..."

The oldest of the pupils tried to reassure him:

"Since we have been with him – we have never seen him fly in the air or make himself seeing and unseen. Perhaps there is a hidden meaning to his words?" And he concluded, in the same persuasive tone: "Be patient, and consider your actions carefully!"

"That is good advice!" the young man agreed with him, the restrained smile in his eyes, that had faded away, flickering again.

The next morning, after a sleepless night on the hard floor of the cave, the guest rose with but one thought in his mind: to return the way he had come.

"I did not come here to learn circus tricks!" he complained, gathering his possessions together. "It is the one truth that I seek, and nothing else!"

"So you're running away then," the oldest pupil observed calmly.

"Call it whatever you like," the young man retorted. "Your teacher is trying to drive me away," he added brusquely.

"Is it our teacher who is driving you away?" asked the oldest pupil in the same measured tone as before – "Or is it the hard floor of the cave?"

For a moment the young man stood still, weighing the words of his host and examining the rocky projections in the floor, that had kept him awake throughout the night.

"I shall stay one week," he declared finally, adding by way of clarification, "to remove the doubt from my heart."

He stayed one week, and then three more weeks – at first enchanted by the silence and the stunning views, and then by the sage himself, by the pure radiance and spiritual fortitude emanating from his every word and gesture. Finally – he sank into prolonged meditation, utterly detached from the passage of time and relieved of his initial doubts.

The seasons passed and the years rolled by.

After eighteen successive years spent in the presence of the teacher – the light flashed and the young man, no longer quite so young – attained enlightenment: the dreams of illusion faded, and the bonds that tied him to the world of appearance were severed, as if they had never been. The one reality, forever constant, shone in his heart with all its splendour, and he knew the truth of endless happiness, and discovered himself an inseparable part of this infinite truth, that is nothing other than perfect freedom.

The former pupil knelt at the feet of his teacher, kissing with his lips the dust at his feet:

"This is all thanks to you, my teacher!" he murmured, beside himself with joy.

"It is not thanks to me, nor to you – rather it is

bestowed by the power of the supreme Grace of which we are all an inseparable part," the teacher declared, with an air of deep gratification, and asked his pupil to stand. They sat side by side and laughed together – clear and resonant, unblemished laughter – the kind that comes from infinite distances and returns to them.

After they had sat thus for a while, with the other pupils joining them in a semi-circle, the former novice turned to the teacher and, still with a broad smile lighting his face, made the observation:

"You promised to teach me to fly in the air and to be seeing and unseen, and this you have not done!"

"I promised, and I kept my promise!"

"How so?" queried the newly enlightened one, and all those present looked curiously at their master.

The old sage replied:

"To fly – means to be freed from weight. The manifestation of this weight is the body – and you are freed from that forever. You also see and you are not seen: it is not within the power of mortals to see you as you are, and you for your part see them – as they are or as they imagine themselves to be – and the choice is yours."

The Worm

A worm announced to the other members of his species that he was tired of the dense darkness under the ground, and he could no longer live here as placidly as he had until now, and he was going to break through the layer of earth enclosing his world and emerge into the wide open spaces, enjoying the warmth and the light of the sun, of which so many had heard – and those upon whom fortune had smiled, had only praise and fulsome admiration for them. And among the older worms there were some who listened attentively to his headstrong and emotive words, and with dignity and sobriety of mind befitting their age, they remarked that his declaration seemed to them a little strange, and to their knowledge there was no place more convenient, more comfortable and more satisfactory for worms than the dense darkness under the ground, under the clods of earth that afford protection from disaster and mayhem and instil confidence in the hearts of the worm population, with their moisture that nourishes on rainy days and is pleasantly cool in the summer's heat. And the oldsters went on to say, in their nasal voices that only worms can hear, that they had heard from their fathers, and they from their fathers' fathers, that any worm who emerges into the daylight, on the exposed surface of the ground, seeking to enjoy the brilliance and the warmth of the sun and experience the wide open spaces – is risking his life. But the worm refused to listen. And the old worms, realising that their words were falling on deaf ears, fell silent and said no more.

The worm dug into the soil, dug tirelessly, with dedication and enthusiasm and prodigious energy, and without respite, and within a short space of time he had extricated himself from the darkness and was crawling over the warm clods of earth, exposed to the glorious brilliance of the rising sun and its caressing, rejuvenating warmth. But instead of enjoying the abundance of light, and happily absorbing the restful warmth, as he had dreamed, and savouring the open spaces to his heart's content, the worm began writhing, there and then, in dreadful pain – dazzled by the light and scorched by the heat, shrivelling, with strength oozing away fast, so that even crawling back into the moist, cool and sheltering depths of the earth was beyond him.

A wasp, contentedly flying and buzzing a hymn of praise to the creator of the world, to the light and the open spaces, and the rising sun, happened to be passing, and saw the worm in his bitter distress. He flew over him, surprised and curious, as he knew the surface of the ground was no place for a worm; what did this one think he was doing, exposing himself to the light of the sun and its lethal heat?

With the last vestiges of his strength, the worm

cried out to the wasp, asking:

"Tell me, flying Sir, why am I being punished so severely, suffering fearful agonies which no words could describe, mortally smitten by the heat of this glorious sun and its light? My end is close at hand. Why?" – the worm repeated in a hoarse and grating voice, a tearful voice.

And the shrewd wasp replied, his voice deep and clear and even:

"It's because you're a worm!"

"Have worms no right to enjoy the heat of the sun and savour its light and feel the freedom of the open spaces?"

"So long as they remain worms – no."

"What must they do then to enjoy, like all other creatures, the freedom of open spaces, the warmth of the sun and its invigorating light?" the worm persisted, and the philosopher wasp replied:

"Stop being worms!"

The Two Brothers

A certain father had two sons. When the time to be gathered to his ancestors was at hand, he divided his property between them. When the father departed from this world the sons buried his body with due reverence, and with the money inherited each acquired a shop for the sale of merchandise. When a year had elapsed, the older brother approached the younger and said to him:

"Come, let us be partners in business, and share equally between us the profit that each of us makes from his shop – as is right and proper between loving brothers."

The younger brother was pleased to hear the other's reasonable suggestion, and he accepted it with a glad heart.

From the day that the partnership between the brothers began and became an established fact, the affairs of the older brother flourished, and his customers grew in number, and his income multiplied many times over. The business of the younger brother, on the other hand, went from bad to worse, and he was not even earning enough to cover his overheads.

As agreed between them, the brothers were combining their profits month by month and dividing them equally.

The wife of the older brother turned to her husband and said to him:

"The profits that your brother is making do not amount to even one tenth of your earnings, and the result is that he is dependent on you and you are the one financing him. He and his family are eating the bread of charity, earned by your sweat and toil. Consider these words of mine and you will find, it is not in accordance with good taste or wisdom – to say nothing of justice – to carry on with a partnership such as this. So talk to your brother and tell him you have decided to dissolve the partnership, which is like a millstone around your neck and the neck of your family. And I am sure, if indeed he is a loyal brother to you, he will take your words in good part and give his consent at once to the dissolution of the partnership. Because," – the wife added – "no upright man can resign himself to dependence on his relative for any length of time, when he is healthy and strong and capable of making a respectable living for himself and his family in any job or profession that he chooses."

The older brother pondered his wife's words, pondered them thoroughly and found there was indeed fairness and good sense in them. He went to his younger brother and told him what his wife wanted him to say, and asked him to agree to the dissolution of the contract.

The younger rose from his seat, held out to the older a steady hand, and then and there he willingly accepted the proposal and the partnership was dissolved.

The brothers parted company and went their separate ways, each to his own shop.

From the day the partnership between the brothers was dissolved, the profits of the older began to diminish: regular customers deserted him and goods rotted in the crates and were discarded for want of buyers.

Soon the older found himself urgently seeking loans at any rate of interest, to cover, if only partially, his mounting losses. It was the opposite case with the younger brother: from the very day that the partnership was dissolved, his business activities flourished and were constantly on the increase, his customers grew in number and his profits multiplied many times over.

Between the older brother and his beloved wife a bitter argument arose – each accusing the other of the lack of foresight that had led to the breaking of the partnership. Now they saw the business of the younger brother prospering while theirs was falling apart; the coffers were empty and all that was left were debts. The creditors were demanding payment and there was nothing to be done to placate them...

While the two of them were arguing between themselves, voices rising high, someone knocked on the door. The older brother went to the door, seething with wrath, and was astonished to find his younger brother standing on the threshold.

"What brings you here?" asked the older, his voice hoarse, eyes still flashing and face tense.

"I thought it right," – the younger began awkwardly – "to offer you the chance of renewing the old partnership. If that's what you want!"

For a long moment the older stood motionless, like one struck by lightning, and the next he held out his arms and clasped his brother in a tight embrace, as tears of happiness welled in his eyes.

So it was that the partnership was renewed.

And then, from the day the agreement was signed, once more the business of the older flourished and prospered, while the business of the younger dwindled and diminished. And when the wife of the older spoke to her husband again about dissolving the partnership he rejected her arguments, declaring it was thanks to the partnership and to the purity of heart of his younger brother that his business was burgeoning, and customers flocking to him in ever greater numbers from day to day, and any harm done to the partnership that had been revived would – first and foremost – harm them: the older brother, his wife and family; this was nothing other than one of the lustrous signs of that higher justice, which human beings are not yet capable of fully comprehending.

Expectations

There was once in the distant past a small country, all of whose inhabitants, to the very last one among them, were renowned for their flawless honesty, their sterling qualities and constant willingness to help others, gladly, in whatever way was required. Needless to say, the people of that distant land had no idea what prisons are, what a judge or a constable looks like.

The black-hearted envoys of evil who were sent, and sent again to this wondrous land invested tireless efforts in sowing dissension and hatred, jealousy and deceit among the inhabitants, to teach them to steal and murder, to cheat and fornicate – and all to no avail.

The black-hearted envoys returned to their senders the way they had come, defeated and depressed, mournful and bare-headed. And their king, with the blackest of all black hearts, choking in his rage, denounced them furiously and commanded they be soundly flogged; some were even hurled into the blazing furnace. But all of this achieved nothing: the inhabitants of that little country continued to stand steadfastly by their honesty and generosity of heart, and to cherish their love of humanity, and to be firm in their willingness to sacrifice themselves for the good of others.

The point was reached where the black-hearted king was forced to summon a meeting of the Supreme Council of Evil, to discuss the matter of that small country. By urgent royal command all the trusted advisers were summoned, from all corners of the earth, from the renowned and the murderous among them to the unknown, who had yet to claim credit for some act of villainy worthy of the name, from the young and the unruly and the hot-headed to the grizzled veterans – with their rich and varied experience of murder and mayhem.

In the long and narrow council chamber, built all of glossy black-marble, with blazing torches of fetid marsh-grass casting a greenish, venomous light into the dingy corners, there were assembled together all the masters of deceit and dishonesty, the paragons of malice and murder from all the lands, in a final attempt to devise an idea of startling spite, worthy of the name, that would put an end once and for all to the irksome and seemingly impregnable virtue of that small country.

The learned deliberations began, every one of those invited taking his turn to speak and putting forward all kinds of ideas, that came highly recommended. The discussions became heated and continued night after night, but as for a solution – there was none.

The highly esteemed members of the council

almost gave up the struggle.

The fury of the black-hearted ruler raged with redoubled force; it was his conviction, based on the reports of reliable spies, that the faith of the inhabitants of that small land was not yet sufficiently crystallised; it was not strong enough to cleanse their hearts utterly from the expectations of this world… and indeed, since time immemorial, those expectations have been in his hands like clay in the hands of the potter, which he manipulates just as he pleases!

On the last night, at the very last moment, before the council dispersed, with no decision taken, there rose from a seat upholstered with the skins of young vipers an elderly individual with forked tail and high and curling horns, who throughout all those long nights of pointless drivel had maintained a silence of ostentatious and superior disdain – and now he had a suggestion of his own to make:

"Let the defeated envoys return to that small country the way that they left it," – he began in a guttural and rasping voice, on his lips a smile of venomous scorn – "but let them change their mode of operation and instead of praising in the most glowing of terms, with all the eloquence that they can muster – every kind of malice and evil instinct, deceit, adultery, theft and murder – let them denounce them explicitly, vehemently, with unequivocal clarity, in public and in private, in all circumstances, whether opportune – or otherwise…"

"By such means we would surely be following in the footsteps of our sworn enemies, joining forces with those who preach at the gates; we shall resemble them utterly!" retorted the black-hearted ruler, in a tone of incomparable ferocity, and in seething indignation he added: "We shall strengthen the power of our enemy instead of weakening it, crushing and destroying it, in accordance with our illustrious tradition and in demonstration of our shining talents, which until this very night have never failed, but have been crowned with spectacular success."

Again this prodigiously elderly man, this one of incomparably rich experience, known in all countries of the world for his malice, that is never dissembled, and for his dissembling that is always malicious, put a sour and arrogant smile on his scarred face, and said with emphatic self-assurance:

"Our sovereign, His Majesty, is quick to anger and therein in his glory; with success that has no peer or equal he has crushed beneath his wicked hooves all the nations of the world except this, this one...but for once, for all the perverse admiration that I feel for this celebrated quality of his, the quality of unbridled anger is not to his credit but on the contrary, it is a fault... So I ask His Majesty to listen to me and weigh patiently what I have to say in conclusion, consider my words carefully and then, if that is his will, he shall make his decision. And I hereby make a solemn undertaking to accept this decision in the spirit and in the letter, for he has no more loyal servant than I, no subject more willing at all times to face any sacrifice, for his glory and for the propagation of his loathsome dominion!"

And because the situation was beyond despair, the black-hearted ruler suppressed his anger, put a twisted smile on his distorted face, and let the old man finish his speech.

For a brief moment the old man with the pock-marked face was silent, a silence intended to accentuate still more the importance that he attached to himself, and then he went on to say:

"In the course of the vehement and unequivocal denunciation, expressed in clear and eloquent language that cannot be misunderstood – those who preach will be asked for living examples of the evils that they are denouncing: How exactly is thieving done, and what is this adultery that you say is rife in other countries? They will not hide anything, not conceal any details... in their meticulous illustrations they will describe everything in living and tangible form, from start to finish... and if there is a need for it, they will demonstrate... to achieve their end they will obviously have recourse to vivid and realistic models, accompanied by unwavering reproof, with the lexicon of words that is appropriate to each of these honourable professions... to show thieving – you will need the thief's lexicon; to show adultery – the adulterer's lexicon; to show murder – the murderer's lexicon; and as for deceit – the agile tongue, wheedling and corrupt, will work wonders... and all of this accompanied by constant, mordant, unequivocal reproof... let our faithful envoys proceed in this manner, and by this venerable, experienced head of mine, I guarantee a successful outcome!"

All those present at the Council of Evil broke into wild laughter, laughter that set the black floors of the palace shaking, on hearing the old man's solemn pledge, a pledge worth less than onion-skin – as worthless in fact as anything that they might say.

And yet they promised the old man, and their promise too was solemn and backed up by lurid and nefarious oaths – that if his advice failed to deliver the results that he promised, he would be ceremoniously immersed in a lake of boiling oil for a term of six hundred and sixty-six years, until he had learned his lesson, learned to babble no more, except to novices who were not yet the devoted retainers of the black-hearted king.

There being no alternative idea, the perverse royal decree was issued, and the envoys hastily returned by the same route to the small country, and adopted their traditional poses – one as a respected parliamentarian, renowned for his flawless integrity, another as a psychologist, another as a journalist, another as an artist; there was a historian too, and a treasury clerk, and a deputy foreign minister and a stockbroker.

And they began the implementation of the new policy, with vigour and with flair.

Soon the envoys of malice and deceit, disguised as reputable men of science, tradesmen, artists, politicians and professionals, became known as the most fervent critics of abhorrent evil, accepting no compromise or pretence and not shying away from demonstrations of genuine wickedness with all the underlying spite and cunning. Nor did they baulk at using the authentic, ambiguous language of evil as an aid to the presentation of vivid and realistic illustration, opening the eyes and penetrating the hearts of all who saw and heard.

A year passed. And in that wondrous land, where the inhabitants had not known the meaning of fraud, theft, adultery or murder – the first thief was caught, soon to be followed by a second; there was a case of fraudulent dealing, and then another, and so on... Suddenly there was the need to establish a police force, and courts and prisons.

Gradually, the small country, known for the rare purity of its ways and its always contented citizens, happy from the dawn of their youth to their last days upon the earth – became like any one of the neighbouring countries, where malice, deceit and adultery had consumed all that was once good. It was the forces of evil that now held sway, ruling without let or hindrance and leading the land from iniquity to iniquity, stifling with hatred, with ruthless cruelty, any aspiration towards honesty, light, truth, loyalty and love.

From the heights of the firmament the ministering angels looked down and saw the wondrous country that had so sadly fallen into the hands of the envoys of evil, and their hearts were grieved. One of the leading angels called together the throngs of his fellows to consider the matter of the disaster that had befallen that nation, and decide whether and how it could be helped, in even the smallest way.

The angels responded to the call of the one set above them, and they assembled on one of the gleaming stars close to the orb of the earth – and when asked, they expressed one after another the firm opinion that the reason for the disaster that had befallen was not the cunning ploys of the powers of darkness, but rather the expectations which the people of that country cherished in their hearts, for the pleasures of this world.

The assembled angels declared unanimously, it was their sacred duty to descend to the little country that was sinking into the mists of barbarism, and do everything possible to reveal to its dejected citizens the true nature of expectations of this world's pleasures. The angels knew that if the inhabitants of this land would only learn to cleanse their hearts from all expectations of worldly pleasure, they would revert to being, as they were before, upright and contented, fearless and generous of heart, loving and loved. And never again would they fall victim to the forces of fraud and deceit.

The angels were as good as their word: they descended to the face of the earth and dispersed among the residents of the small land that had once been renowned throughout the world for the purity of its ways, to try to make them understand the scale of the impending disaster – the effect of cherishing expectations of worldly pleasures. And to this very day angels are at work among the inhabitants of the small country, with great energy and remarkable patience.

And whosoever hears the words of the angels and takes them to heart, and detaches himself utterly from expectations of the world's pleasures, will once again become happy, strong-minded and generous of heart, loving and loved; whereas the one who does not accept the words of the angels and is subject to the malign influence of the forces of evil – remains gloomy and dejected, bitterly bemoaning his life and trembling in fear of his imminent and inevitable death.

The Sultan and Destiny

In the fair city of Constantinople, in one of the markets teeming with men and beasts, in a remote corner near the cess-pit, sat a man dressed in rags, reckoned wise but unfortunate.

All kinds of tales were told about the remarkable wisdom of the man, his astute counsels, his ability to make peace between sworn enemies with a tasteful word, spoken in the right tone and at the right time.

Needless to say, the traders in the great market were his chief admirers, and when they were in trouble they were not ashamed to go down to the stinking place where he sat, to seek and to find a solution to the problems facing them.

But although they all wished him well and respected him, and did not tire of working on his behalf, he was unable to hold on to any kind of business or craft which would have earned him a respectable income, allowing him to know something of the pleasures of life – the birthright of all flesh. Everything the man touched – slipped away through his fingers as if it never was. If one of the traders took him on as an assistant or a partner, the business immediately began to fail: profits dwindled and merchandise rotted, unsold, and the benefactor was forced – on the verge of bankruptcy – to rid himself of his employee or partner.

This happened not once, and not twice. The gold coins donated to him by a generous burgher disappeared from his pocket almost before they were in it. Sometimes he was given clothes, ordered specially for him by anonymous patrons – and they were stained with filth that very day or torn the day after, such that nothing remained of their former glory and their eye-catching splendour.

"Poor, luckless man!" his well-wishers sighed – and abandoned their fruitless attempts to make life easier for him in some way. And it seemed that the man himself was reconciled to his nickname and to his bitter lot. He used to come every morning, help with setting up some stall or other, receiving in exchange a piece of fruit or a loaf of bread that had been left out in the sun a whole week and turned as hard as board, go back to his place beside the cess-pit and calmly consume his meal.

In the afternoon, when hunger assailed him, the man would rise from his seat and do the rounds of the stalls, helping anyone who needed help, ordering a cup of steaming coffee for a busy trader and serving it himself – getting in return a cracked pitta bread, a few morsels of meat or cold stew, and sometimes – a sliver of rancid goat's cheese and a rotten apple for dessert.

No one tried any longer to improve his condition. And if a new trader happened to be there, one who had just now rented his stall and refurbished it, and "Luckless" helped him with good and useful advice, till the trader swore in his heart he would make every effort to release him from his dire state – his fellow stallholders would approach him, with his best interests at heart, and earnestly warn him of the consequences. If for all this he persisted – then "Luckless" himself would come and reject his generous offers.

And because the stories about him did not come to an end but on the contrary, blossomed and flourished, with a little "seasoning" added – the man chose, as we said before, to sit not far from the mouth of the cess-pit, where the vile stench could be relied upon to deter the curious, those eager to feast their mocking eyes on him.

Everyone loves a story – and none more so than municipal officers and enlightened rulers. And so it was that the story of the luckless sage went around and came to the ears of the Sultan, who in those days saw the fair city of Constantinople as his sole capital and dwelt there surrounded by a veritable entourage of ministers and advisers, guardsmen with well-ironed uniforms and courtiers with well-ironed tongues.

The Sultan was intrigued to hear the strange stories, and since there were no wars raging at the time to tax his towering intellect, no cases of embezzlement on the part of minions which demanded his personal attention – he rose one day and demanded that he be taken to the market, to see the unlucky sage for himself.

In the royal court there was uproar, such as had not been known since the day the Sultan's father threw his grandfather's wives and concubines into the sea. Carriages were brought out from neglected mews and the dust of ages – undisturbed since the wars of the Sultan's great-grandfather – was swept from them. Wheels were oiled, carpets beaten and seats padded. Where the moth had left his distinctive calling-card and this could not be ignored, cushions were laid – a veritable mountain of cushions, embroidered with threads of silver and gold. The Sultan planted his pampered limbs amid these cushions and escorted by an impressive retinue – made all speed to the market.

Horsemen who went ahead to clear the way for the Sultan alarmed the traders, and they were even more alarmed when these horsemen flatly refused to accept any of the bakshish offered to them.

"The Day of Reckoning has come!" – the stallholders trembled as they pondered in their fevered brains all those taxes that had not been paid or had been "forgotten", in return for all kinds of gifts presented to the demure wives of tax-gatherers. In those days, for either of these two offences, the clever and upright man could expect the unique, once-in-a-lifetime privilege of seeing this beautiful world through the noose of the hangman's rope, nicely soaped.

The traders came running to "Luckless" the sage and asked for his advice. He wiped the gloomy expression from his worn face and said, with a half-smile:

"If this were the Day of Reckoning, the Sultan would not have bothered to come to the market in person. He would have sent his executioners and tax-gatherers, rather than soil his dainty hands with your merchandise, or tickle his nostrils with the fragrance of strong garlic and old onions."

"What, then, brings the Sultan here so suddenly?" the traders persisted, somewhat reassured, as the sage's words on this occasion were not without reason.

"Entertainment!" – declared "Luckless", and he added: "If there were a fire-eater or a sword-swallower amongst you, I would tend to believe he had come for that reason, but since there is no such performer here, I can only suppose he has heard some story about me and has made haste to come and see me – while I still live..."

As he was still speaking the Sultan's minions arrived and dragged him to the middle of the market square where the Sultan's great carriage stood, its paint peeling, like a ship aground on a sandbank, all its masts ripped away by hurricane winds.

Gendarmes stood around, and a dense crowd gathered among the market-stalls, uttering not a sound.

The luckless sage was led to the lowest step at the door of the royal carriage where he bowed down low, and prostrated himself on the ground, and did not rise until given permission. Then he looked up and saw the rosy face of the Sultan, floating above a mountain of cushions.

"They tell strange stories about you," the ruler began, in a thin, confident voice: "You are described as the greatest sage of this generation – and yet, as a man of incomparable misfortune. I want to hear with my own ears and see with my own eyes, and check the truth of the stories they tell." And without a moment's hesitation, the ruler asked from his vantage point on the heaped cushions:

"Is destiny a real thing?"

And at once the reply came:

"It is no more a real thing than the wind is a real thing."

"How so?" – the Sultan leaned forward, his interest aroused.

"The wind, as you know, is air; and yet it has the power to tear up trees from their roots, shake the foundations of houses, divert ships at sea and capsize them."

The answer pleased the royal visitor.

"You are wise indeed!" – he declared – "But on the subject of destiny, I disagree with you. Destiny is an illusion, an invention of idle and dim-witted cowards. They call you 'Luckless'. From this day forward you shall be known as 'Lucky'."

"How is that?" asked the sage, and for all his sober wisdom – his voice shook and his eyes flashed with sparks of childish hope.

"Take this stick!" – the ruler handed him a thick walking-stick, a work of true craftsmanship, and continued: "Go and stand at the end of the street, down there. Raise the stick and throw it away from you, along the street: from the place where you stand to the point where the stick lands, all the buildings, apartments, shops and stores – will be yours!"

With trembling hands the luckless sage took the Sultan's stick.

The crowd, which had listened enraptured to every word and syllable uttered by the sovereign, held its breath.

"Luckless" approached the end of the street and looked along it: an array of fine buildings, spacious shops and stalls laden with all good things – and all waiting to welcome him.

The sage waved the stick above his head, swung it around several times with all his strength, to add further momentum to the throw, and he hurled it away from him, along the broad street, gleaming in the summer sunlight, smiling at him and promising him release from penury, and affluence beyond his wildest dreams.

The stick, flung with tremendous, almost superhuman force, hit a solid stone bollard, rebounded and pierced the wide-open eye of the luckless sage.

There is no such thing as destiny, but this sage is certainly doomed to misfortune! – the shrewd ruler mused inwardly – and gave the signal to his escorts.

With a strident creaking the royal carriage left the market square, which soon returned to its customary tumult.

The luckless sage earned another nickname: "Cyclops".

The Barber of Mecca

In the city of Mecca, where the majority of the citizens make their livelihood from pilgrims, there lived, by the grace of Allah, Mahfuz the barber.

Mahfuz was renowned as a skilful barber, a conscientious worker giving satisfaction to even the most exacting of customers. Pilgrims arriving, having heard his praises sung by those returning, came to him in hordes in the hectic days of the Haj, to be shaved and to have their hair trimmed. No wonder then, that at these times there was always a long queue of customers waiting. But in the other seasons of the year, Mahfuz had neither work nor livelihood, and he lived in penury. Had he not saved a little from the times of Haj, he would have sunk to the demeaning depths of starvation, and this because the residents of Mecca, the decisive majority at least – were not among his customers. There were reasons for this, the best-known being – the nature of the "salon" of Mahfuz and its location.

The "salon" had two round chairs: one with a back, where the customer sat for the barber's ministrations, while on the other – without a back – sat the next in line. The other customers stood or sat – according to preference – on the solid and sacred ground of glorious Mecca. The ceiling of the "salon" invariably consisted of the endless and usually cloudless skies of Allah the Merciful.

Mahfuz had a polished mirror, set in a steel frame, which he was adept at placing, skilfully, on any hook or stone projecting from a peeling and misshapen wall. Sometimes, in the absence of such facilities, the broad back of one of the customers served as an improvised support for this mirror. The other tools of the barber's trade Mahfuz kept in a little cylindrical case, made of thick and hairy camel-hide, proof against rain, sun, sand and wind. Mahfuz was a bachelor, because he could never afford to pay the bride-price even for some hunch-backed drudge of a redundant maidservant.

Time passed and one bright day during the Haj, when the barber's stall was set up at the southern end of the market, teeming with pilgrims, and the queue of customers was as long and sinuous as the primeval serpent, and on the chair with the back sat Halil Abu Daud, one of the best-known grandees of Rabat – Mahfuz was approached by a beggar-dervish, his clothes dusty and threadbare, his beard lank – asking to have his hair trimmed.

Without a word Mahfuz pulled the towel from Halil's neck, wiped the soap bubbles from his beard and signalled to him to stand up from his seat and move to the backless chair, which was vacated for him. And while the wealthy man from Rabat fumed, bewildered by this treatment, Mahfuz sat the dervish down in the backed chair, soaped his beard, shaved him meticulously, trimmed his hair and refused to accept the coppers that the other held out to him.

Moved by this gesture, the dervish vowed to give Mahfuz the first donation deposited in his collecting-box.

The dervish made his way to the market-place, holding out his collecting-box to the passers-by. At a corner, far from the tumult of the Haj, he encountered a woman with veiled face, who put in his hand a nugget of gold, a thing of great value. The dervish hurried back to the fringes of the market, found Mahfuz the barber and put the gold nugget in his hand.

"Isn't it possible, in the name of Allah and his Prophet, to give charity anymore?" Mahfuz protested. He took the nugget and put it in the outstretched hand of a blind beggar, who was feeling his way through the crowd with a long stick.

The King and the Birds

In a certain land there lived an eccentric king, who sometimes saw things in an unusual way and took action accordingly: issuing commands, formulating policies and imposing legislation.

One night the king could not sleep; despite all his efforts and the efforts of his physician and his wise counsellors – even closing his eyes was beyond him. This irked him a great deal. The king had important and urgent matters of state to consider the next day – how could he do this, if worn out and weary from prolonged and painful insomnia?

But a little before dawn, restful sleep came to him finally. The king closed his eyes, glad at heart and relieved in spirit, knowing that in spite of everything he would be fit to fulfil his obligations to his realm and to his people.

The garden of the royal palace, with its coppices of ornamental trees and its rare and colourful flowers, its well-tended and verdant lawns, stretching from horizon to horizon – was thronged with early-rising birds, whose singing is sweet to the ears of all.

That fateful morning, the raucous squabbling of the birds drowned out their sweeter and more melodious tunes – and their harsh screeches woke the king again and drove the last vestiges of sleep from his eyelids.

The light slumber, that had brought him such relief, disappeared as if it had never been.

The king leapt from his bed in a rage, summoned his secretaries and at once dictated a hasty edict, in the following terms:

"Within a week from today, all the birds of this kingdom are to be hunted down, destroyed and exterminated, such that no trace or remnant of them is left. And this because..." – the king thought it appropriate to give a reason – "they have absolutely no conception of, or aspiration towards, what is good and true and beautiful, although some learned people of this generation, in their utter intellectual blindness, attribute such qualities to them. They are obsessed, when all is said and done, with noisy, discordant and irritating argument over a few miserable crumbs or seeds, which are supplied to them in abundance, or over places to build nests – and there is no lack of these either. Everything they do is founded in falsehood, deceit and trickery, and they never pause to wonder if their singing brings relief and comfort to those who hear it or bitter despair and dejection – does it soothe to sleep or does it drive sleep away from the weary eyelids!"

The order was displayed, as was customary in those times, on the information-boards designed for this purpose, and it was proclaimed time and time again by the royal heralds, to the accompaniment of drums and trumpets, in all corners of the realm.

Immediately, gangs of hunters were recruited, to chase down and destroy indiscriminately all the birds they could find, shooting them down with arrows as they flew in the air or perched on roofs and trees, walked on the ground or hid in their nests.

Within a week the kingdom was purged of all winged creatures, and then the borders were placed under heavy guard, to catch any bird that might try to cross over, by design or by accident. And the watchmen performed their task most effectively and gradually the birds too came to realise that they must avoid these borders if they wanted to stay alive.

The kingdom was quiet then, with no more of the pleasant trilling or the cheerful chirping of birds, or the beating of wings – powerful or gentle; hard to imagine that any land could be so quiet.

The eccentric king did not suffer any more from insomnia; on the contrary he slept soundly and recouped his energy and went about his royal business with vim and efficiency.

Every morning the king would rise from his bed, alert and invigorated, stand at his window, and look out at his spacious and luxuriant gardens, under the strange pall of shaded silence, the bright light of the sun in the blue skies and wispy clouds, as pure as angels' wings, drifting across them serenely, with the delight of ages past

Days passed, and weeks and months.

One morning, when the king rose from his bed and peered as usual through his window at his cherished gardens, to melt in the tranquil gold and silver foliage of his trees, delight in the stunning contrasts in the colours of his flowers, breathe in the invigorating freedom of his well-tended lawns, stirring gently in the balmy breeze – how great was the surprise, turning quickly to bewilderment and from bewilderment to horror – when instead of the gold and silver foliage, the flowers filling the void with their delicate fragrances and lawns stretching away to the far horizons – his eyes saw nothing but blackened tree trunks, naked and ugly, withered flowers and hard, dull-coloured earth.

In his alarm and his bitter despair the king demanded that the most eminent scientists in the kingdom be brought before him at once, to enquire into this phenomenon and explain to him exactly, in meticulous detail, just what was happening here. And if, which heaven forbid, this was not a passing natural phase but there was a malicious hand in it – the investigators of crime would take charge, and uncover the culprit or culprits who would be hanged without delay in the central square of the capital city.

The specialists in the natural sciences were summoned from the four corners of the kingdom and they came in haste to the palace of the king; all of them – to the last one among them, were men of repute and worldwide renown.

The experts deliberated, inquired and analysed, probed everything thoroughly, and they overlooked nothing; not a single detail escaped their keen, vigilant eyes. The experts drew their learned conclusions, and finally stood before the king and said to him:

"O King, live forever! The reason for the sudden withering and the lethal decay that have spread through the royal gardens and outside them as well, have blighted every plant in the kingdom and are already showing themselves in neighbouring countries too – is nothing but the unrestrained increase in the population of worms. The direct and indirect cause of this unrestrained increase is the total absence of birds within the borders of the kingdom.

"The birds, it is true, did not pay proper homage to the King, and their song – sometimes turning into a raucous and quarrelsome shriek – disturbed his sleep and was liable to make him fail in his hallowed obligations to his people and his land; but the departure of the birds has naturally meant that the worms, which in the past did not dare emerge from their holes, have moved in to fill the void that has been left... they have eaten and consumed to their hearts' content... and overnight everything has collapsed and vanished from sight as if it never was..."

And the scholars went on to explain:

"The worms are celebrating throughout the kingdom and outside it as well, and on everything they touch they have left their limp, wormish stamp. Many of the King's subjects already believe that the worms have wisdom, and lessons can be learned from them – and they are becoming like worms themselves...

"Unlike the birds, the worms have not the slightest spark of any interest in what is good, beautiful and true. The opposite is the case: they utterly despise the good and the beautiful and the true, and their entire vocation is a constant effort to attack and undermine the good and the beautiful and the true, and if it were only possible – to destroy them and bring about their final end.

"In times past the presence of birds led to the proliferation of poets and lovers and heroes, people of high repute, of virtue and principle.

"In our time, the effect of the worms has been to render those of high repute and principle ridiculous in the eyes of all; and the mob will scorn them, hate them and expel them, eager to pay respect to the worms alone and doing everything possible to resemble them...

"And in all likelihood it is too late now to bring the birds back to the dying kingdom, since they have learned to recognise its borders and to keep well away from it and beware of its skilled hunters, and they pass on this dire warning to their offspring – not only by way of parable but in the guts as well, an atavistic memory. And meanwhile, the law of the worms is gaining converts outside the borders of the realm as well and is going from strength to strength, without needing any help from the worms themselves. People infect one another with wormishness, and are quickly wormified. Terrible danger threatens the future of the world and of all humanity."

On hearing these grim words, in bitter despair the king rent his fine and regal clothing, put on sackcloth and scattered ashes over his head, and vowed to fast and to mortify himself, and torment his body and mind and not desist from prayer and supplication until he should be forgiven, and his people and all other peoples be granted at least a glimpse of salvation...

Sure enough, the king's privations, his vows and his prayers did avail him – but only him and the members of his household and his entourage, those who were unreservedly loyal to him and followed in his footsteps and did exactly as he did, putting on sackcloth and scattering ashes over their heads, tormenting their minds and mortifying their bodies, praying and pleading without a pause and turning away, with earnest repentance, from the law of the worms that was eating away at all hearts...

The other subjects of the kingdom, who had embraced the law of the worms, which declares that lofty ideals and principles are merely obstacles to the pleasure inherent in gnawing at another's heart, and this is the one and the only pleasure that exists in the world – were munching away at one another with determination and persistence, till all that remained of them was a vile stench, poisoning the air of their abode.

Finding the stench unbearable, the king and his retainers fled from the kingdom while they still could, and left it forever.

And to this day they are still wandering and roaming the wide open spaces of the world, bemoaning the bitterness of their fate and warning people against the law of the worm and the wormification that follows it, bringing ruin and destruction to those who wormify themselves and leaving no trace of them. But no one listens to them or hears their voices and the law of the worm spreads and prevails over all, and there is no one who will dare stand against it and resist it. And one after the other, kingdoms and states and peoples and nations fall victim to it. And the king is beside himself with grief, seeing what he is seeing and hearing what he is hearing, as indeed are the members of his family and his retinue. And they are driven away with contempt and abuse from every state or nation where they attempt to set foot, and they are spurned by all mankind. And the world, having surrendered unconditionally to the law of the worm, and becoming ever more wormified, is advancing before their eyes towards the dreadful destruction, from which there is no deliverance.

The Best of the Best

One of the kings of ancient times, among the most highly esteemed of them all, a warrior and a hero, grew tired of conquering the territories and slaughtering the armies and the citizenry of neighbouring kingdoms, and resolved to devote himself instead to the pursuit of pure wisdom. He invited to his sumptuous and spacious palace all those renowned for outstanding intellect, all those acquainted with the secret lore of the cosmos, anyone who having studied pure wisdom was qualified to teach the subject.

The halls of the place were thronged with solemn-faced individuals, bald-headed, bearded and bewhiskered, keen-eyed men whom God in His infinite grace had endowed with tongues not to be silenced by day nor restrained by night.

From time to time the king, the seeker after pure wisdom, convened well-attended meetings, meetings noted for their impassioned debates on the subject of the roots, the manifestations and the achievements of pure wisdom.

Differences of opinion, though expressed in the most refined of language, were acute, polarised and remained firmly held throughout the duration of these august gatherings. On one issue only were all disagreements set aside and all participants unanimous, all those scholars of spectacular intellect, consumers of the king's bounty: the golden age of pure wisdom would come into being only through the agency of an enlightened king, our king in other words, the wisest of all kings – its most steadfast pursuer and most assiduous devotee.

At one of these erudite assemblies, two conflicting theories were raised regarding the true origin of pure wisdom. The sages of that generation were divided into two rival camps, equal in the numbers of their supporters, in the vehemence of their arguments, in the acuity of their expressions and in their obstinacy, their determination not to countenance any attempt at compromise. One camp saw truth as the one and exclusive foundation for the growth and the prosperity of pure wisdom, whose golden age, as we know, will come into being only through the agency of a wise king, our king in other words, may God preserve him, make him mighty and rout his enemies before him and lengthen his days; the other camp, on the contrary, held un-truth to be the exalted, the one and only foundation for the growth and prosperity of pure wisdom, whose golden age, as we know, will come into being only through the agency of a wise king, our king in other words, may God preserve him, make him mighty and rout his enemies before him and lengthen his days.

Since the two camps stood their ground with determination impervious to any kind of logical analysis, with implacable hostility and unwillingness to consider even the slightest of concessions – they turned to the king, to serve as judge between them and final arbiter.

The king responded to their appeal and organised an experiment which in his opinion was bound to put an end once and for all to the impassioned controversies – those smooth tongues consuming all the good things that the palace had to offer. The experiment was intended to provide an unequivocal answer to the vital question: is it truth or untruth, or both of them together, or neither of them – which form the basis of pure wisdom.

The king issued a decree, according to which any person, irrespective of sex, race, nationality or religion – could ask him a question or inform him of something, and if the king were forced to say, in reply to the question or in response to the information, that the words of the questioner or the informant were based on lies – that person would receive two sacks of gold coins. The duration of the experiment – three years from the day of the announcement.

The palace was in uproar: the maids of honour of the queen's entourage murmured, the sages were perplexed, while the populace looked on with bemused interest. The wisdom of the wisest king of any generation was eloquently expressed in his decree.

First to appear before the king were the sages of his court, the consumers of his bounty – in their thousands. The answers to their questions and the responses to their information took up the whole of the first year. Not one of them succeeded in inducing the king to say: "Your words, my esteemed sage, are based on a lie!" – or words to that effect. The failure of his sages was no less a disappointment to the king himself, who began to see as a waste the prodigious sums spent every month on their salaries.

In the wake of the court sages came alumni of the various academies, colleges of the sciences and schools of the arts, psychologists of all kinds and distinguished ministers from neighbouring states which had signed treaties of peace and goodwill with His Majesty's government.

They too achieved nothing. To every one of their questions, even those couched in the most eloquent terms, the king would reply with a broad smile: "I have heard of such a thing" or, "That is indeed possible". And to every piece of information imparted to him he responded brightly: "Such things are liable to happen!"

So the second year passed and the king was not outwitted, and his experiment seemed set fair to prove what it was supposed to prove – what the king knew in his heart that the experiment was ultimately going to prove.

In the third year the royal palace was besieged by

advisors of all kinds: secret advisors and tax advisors, military advisors and economic advisors, ethical and religious consultants, political counsellors, specialists in entertainment and bodily health, advisors of advisors. And when they too failed to attain their objective – distinguished soldiers tried to win the sacks of gold, and they were followed in their turn by athletes of renown and circus performers, artists and craftsmen. Then came the peddlers, fortune-tellers, cardsharpers, beggars.

The third year was drawing to a close, with the king's victory imminent and menacing, as there was no knowing how things would transpire in the aftermath of such a decisive victory: would he eject from the palace all the illustrious sages and save the state treasury a great deal of money? Or would he go further and call to account all those dependent on his bounty and at the same time – return to warfare against those lands with whom he had yet to sign binding peace treaties.

The situation was fluid and prone to surprises of unknown nature, intensity and scope. An obscure sense of worry, incomprehensible and yet – justified, took up residence in the hearts of all.

The last day of the experiment arrived. In fact – the last half day: the experiment had begun at noon precisely, and according to the edict it was to end on the same day, three years on, at the same hour – noon precisely.

The king sat on his gigantic throne, with its ornate gilding and trappings, its inlay of precious stones – at the end of the palace concourse, which in the past had served as the setting for ceremonial parades but in recent years had been utterly neglected; wild grass was springing up between the paving stones. The king sat and waited for questioners to arrive. The concourse, some half a parasang in length, was deserted.

The king's eminent sages sat in the sumptuous halls of the palace with their fittings of gold and silver – mournful and bareheaded, while from time to time a heavy sigh emerged from between clenched teeth, this being nothing other than resignation to fate and nostalgic longings for the not so distant past. Other courtiers hid in their rooms, in gloomy anticipation of the future. The simple folk dispersed to their own concerns, and no longer came to feast their eyes on the subtle questioners, eliciting apt responses from the wisest of kings.

The queen gave instructions that the gates of the palace were to be closed at eleven o'clock and forty-five minutes, as the distance from the gates to the majestic throne at the end of the concourse could be covered by a brisk walker in a quarter of an hour.

This order on the part of the queen (later to be described as "arbitrary") provoked some acute controversy: did the royal edict make it absolutely clear – from both ethical and legal perspectives – whether the times in question referred to standing before the royal seat, or appearing at the gates of the palace? In the opinion of most of the king's eminent sages, clutching at straws, it was arrival at the gates that was meant. Any wayfarer, appearing at the palace gates at twelve noon – would be fully entitled to pose questions or to impart information.

The queen was displeased but the wise king accepted the interpretation of his sages – although his thin, meaningful smile set their hearts quaking.

The concourse, half a parasang in length, was still deserted.

At the gate stood the guardsmen, in uniforms which used to be resplendent, in the days when the soldier held a position of respect in the palace – but which were now showing signs of serious neglect: oil-stains and buttons missing or loose, patches sewn in place with threads not matching the colour of the original garment. This attire was incapable of arousing the kind of admiration tinged with reverence that it was originally supposed to arouse.

The big precision hand of the pendulum clock suspended above the king's head was approaching the smaller, thicker hand which was already pointing, unruffled as ever, to the figure 12... The sages, peering out from amid the gaudy marble pillars of the palace, held their breath. And before they had time to expel the air that was in danger of exploding their lungs – the larger hand, unaware of the significance of the occasion, had joined the smaller. The well-oiled mechanism of the royal clock, that sophisticated feat of technology, sprang into action, and all were tensed in anticipation of the twelve pellucid chimes, which would resonate for a further half-second in the dense atmosphere. And then – just as the last half-second was passing, as will come as no surprise to those familiar with the conventions of the fairy-tale – a crumpled figure appeared at the palace gates and stood on the threshold.

From the outset, it was clear there was nothing in such a figure calculated to bring relief and deliverance to the eminent sages, consumers of the king's bounty, or to the populace whose taxes subsidised this largesse. However – there escaped from the dry throats of the sages, clustered in the rooms of the palace, a spontaneous, somewhat ragged cry of "Hurrah!" This cry surprised not only the king but also those who had uttered it, devoid as it was of reason and logic.

The king, growing impatient meanwhile, sent a chariot to meet the guest and bring him forward with all possible speed. And so it was that before the echoes of the limpid chimes of the clock had died away – the chariot returned and deposited before the king a man of no style or substance whatsoever: his lank hair grew wild, his clothes were patched and crumpled, his beard thick, eyes small – and smiling, with a childish and bashful air.

"Who are you?" asked one of the guardsmen.

"A breeder of donkeys from the north," the other replied.

The man bowed before his king and asked his pardon for having almost arrived too late:

"I had to clean the stable," he apologised with an air of unease, before adding in a more confident tone: "But as you see, fate willed it, and here I am!" The donkey breeder repeated his deep bow, and while doing so laid at the feet of the king two empty sacks, large sacks made of pigskin.

"What are these for?" asked the king, amused.

"These are the sacks that you must fill with gold coins!" – the answer came promptly.

"Why should I do that?" the king queried, puzzled but still amused.

"Because your late father, may he rest in peace, borrowed two sacks full of gold coins from my grandmother."

"That is a lie!" cried the king, deeply affronted.

"Then you lose your wager and you must pay."

"What you say is absolutely true!" the wise king corrected himself hurriedly, before it was too late.

"Then you must repay the debt!" the donkey breeder smiled, a restrained and innocent smile.

There was a long, and deep silence in the palace.

The king stood facing the donkey breeder open-mouthed, shaken and perplexed to the root of his soul.

A few moments passed. Once he had recovered, he ordered that the sacks be filled with gold coins and when this was done, he turned to the donkey breeder and declared solemnly:

"The experiment that I devised did not turn out well. You are a wiser man than I am," and leaning towards him he asked: "Can you tell me from where you acquired this remarkable wisdom?"

"From the donkeys, Your Majesty," the man replied, and explained: "From the braying sounds they make I can tell which donkey is a good bet, commanding a decent market price and worth the effort of raising, and which is inferior, of poor value and not worth the effort. When your decree came to my attention, I knew that the offer on the table was the very best of the best, and well worth the effort of coming here!" the donkey breeder concluded, and having bowed deeply and politely he loaded the sacks, filled with coins of pure gold, onto the chariot waiting for him and asked the driver to take him away from the palace.

Immediately after his departure, the king ordered the expulsion from his palace of all the sages. Shortly after this he gave up dabbling in pure wisdom, and took up warfare again. And when he was asked by one of his ministers what was the reason for this abrupt change, he replied simply:

"Better a warrior king than a smart-arse donkey!"

The blind and the Sighted

In a remote corner of the world, there existed a community of people all of whom, young and old alike, had been born blind, and of whom the decisive majority remained blind until death. The very tiniest of minorities among the blind in that remote corner of the world enjoyed the gift of sight, and this after climbing a high mountain under the guidance of a sighted person and reaching a sacred spring, whose clear waters had the faculty of opening the eyes of the blind. The journey to the spring was long and arduous, and those who attempted it and completed it successfully were few indeed. Furthermore, a sighted guide was not easily to be found, and not every aspirant could call upon the services of such a person.

The detailed accounts written by those who had succeeded in reaching the sacred spring, whose eyes had been opened to the light for which they longed – were kept by the blind in their hallowed books, written in a special script consisting of projections and indentations on thick paper. But the community of the blind did not always have the leisure to study these sacred texts, which had accumulated over the years. Sometimes the effort seemed pointless and without profit. What is the purpose, they asked, of learning about the beauty of the land and the heights of the heavens, the limpid waters of a mountain stream or the sheen of the mighty sea, the powerful and invigorating light of the sun – so long as the way to the spring that opens the eyes of the blind is so complicated, and a guide for the journey so hard to find?

The days passed, and the blind went about their daily routine, groping and feeling their way and with a heavy sense of dejection in their hearts, as ever. And then it happened that to one of the families a son was born who was not only blind, like his parents and his parents' parents, and their parents before them, but also lame in one leg. When the disabled lad grew up, he did not go out with his relatives, neighbours and friends to their varied and various pursuits and did not work as they did, but stayed at home – bored. And having no other choice, the boy began studying the holy books, scanning the texts over and over again, until the picture of the world outside was painted before his eyes with wondrous clarity, as if it stood before him in all its vivid colours, living and breathing. It was not long before, under the influence of the books that he read, the cripple began imagining to himself he was no longer blind but on the contrary, he could see – and see all that the sighted had seen in their time and described at length in their books, and his vision was even superior, being more acute than theirs.

The cripple did not stay idle for long. He stood up in a public place and told the people he was no longer blind but could see – everything in full breadth and length and height and depth – and he described before all those who were inclined to listen the wondrous sights that he had supposedly seen, in meticulous detail, garnished here and there with the fruits of his imagination.

In the grip of amazement and reverent fear, his audience lost no time telling neighbours, relatives and friends, telling them the incredible story of the blind cripple, praising and extolling him in the most fulsome terms.

The blind cripple went from strength to strength, delivering sensational lectures in which he not only recounted the vivid descriptions that he had gleaned from various holy books, but also declared with force and conviction that his predecessors had not precisely gained the light, and did not quite see what they saw in the fullness of depth, breadth, height and width. Everything described by the ancients – the cripple added with fiery emphasis – was but a fraction of the whole, a tiny and negligible particle. This was not all: by virtue of his extraordinarily acute, full and genuine vision, unlike the defective vision of his predecessors – he knew another way to open eyes, by a quite different method, a short and a quick one compared with that hazardous journey to the mountains and the sacred spring, in the company of a guide whose own sight was far from perfect. But before he would reveal the secret of the good and the easy and the genuine way, those who wished to gain the gift of sight under his tutelage must obey him in every respect, serve him properly and never cast doubt on his pronouncements. Furthermore, it was declared that anyone who failed to comply with his commands, whether he wanted to be sighted or had decided to forego the privilege it made no difference – his fate would be the same: roasting for all eternity in the furnaces of Hell. He, by virtue of his remarkable and perfect vision, could clearly see those furnaces, and he could even make out, among the flames, all those who had described their experiences in books, having climbed to that spring and supposedly gained sight.

The blind inhabitants of that remote corner of the world were confused, and their heavy weight of dejection grew heavier still – a thousand times worse than before. But they were left with no choice and they tried to follow the instructions of the cripple, who was claiming that his was the only true sight, beyond any level of eyesight previously attained in this universe. And disasters were not slow in coming, and many blind folk fell into the crevices and pits that surrounded the township and perished, while obeying the instructions of the cripple. But no one dared cast doubt on his statements or query his vision.

And it came about that a man happened to be passing through this place, a man whose eyes were truly open, and he understood immediately the dreadful predicament into which the blind people had been plunged, through following the leadership of the blind cripple.

He sought out the cripple and admonished him, saying he clearly saw the disaster that he was bringing down on his flock; the man should admit the error of his ways, express some public remorse and put an end to this dangerous state of affairs. But the cripple responded to him with violence and abuse, inciting the mob against him and having him thrown into jail.

Days passed, and the blind cripple, his status unimpaired by disasters, and the members of his flock following him and believing everything he said, as befits the blind – declared that the time had come to go up to the spring of deliverance which, unlike that distant spring, at the end of a long and tortuous path and endowing its visitors with nothing better than defective vision – gave to those who bathed their eyes in it the same perfect vision that he enjoyed.

This surprising announcement evoked a highly emotional response on the part of the man's audience. There and then an impressive procession set out, in which the whole of the community of those blind from birth took part, with the single exception of the prison guard, who on account of his advanced age had decided to forego the opportunity of obtaining perfect vision.

From the narrow window of his cell the sighted one

followed everything that was happening outside. He saw the leader limping along at the head of his procession, rounding the corner of a rocky cliff and advancing towards a great dark chasm.

From the prison the sighted man shouted a warning, telling them of the abyss gaping at their feet.

The cripple turned and responded to him with savage abuse and an arrogant laugh, then stepped forward, lost his footing and plunged headlong into the abyss, disappearing from sight. He was closely followed by his obedient flock, paying no heed to the warning of the sighted one.

Thus the community of the blind from birth was wiped out by the blind cripple who claimed to have perfect vision, and no trace or residue was left of it, other than the elderly prison guard, who released the sighted one from detention so he could tell the sad story of his blind fellow citizens. He himself died shortly afterwards.

The Girl and the Butterflies

There once was a girl who loved butterflies dearly, of all kinds, sizes and colours.

The girl's home was situated in the heart of open fields and because most of her time was her own, as with all girls of her age, she used to leave the house every morning, run in the fields and search out among the colourful flowers the butterflies that she loved so much, chasing them and catching them with a little net designed for this purpose. A butterfly caught by her enjoyed the very same treatment as that meted out by scientists with a professional interest in butterflies – being fastened with a shining steel pin to a broad, polished wooden board, classified according to size and colour.

Needless to say, the butterflies did not respond to the girl with reciprocal affection, or thank her for the systematic scientific treatment which robbed them of their freedom, caused them pain, starved them and doomed them to a slow death on a hard and unsympathetic wooden board.

The acute suffering of the butterflies, their grief, and their silent protests came to the attention of the guardian angel of butterflies, who came at once to their aid.

The angel took on the form of a young woman, with pleasant features and deep blue eyes, reflecting all the goodwill in the world, and went into the green field and met the girl walking on one of the picturesque paths. The disguised angel greeted the butterfly hunter cordially and asked what she was doing. And when the girl spoke of her intense love of butterflies, the attractive young woman commented that anyone who loves any creature, such as a butterfly for example, should do everything possible for the happiness of that creature and do it no harm – least of all, cause it pain and untimely death.

The girl smiled and told the young lady with the marvellous, lustrous eyes that she could not resist the power of her impulses, her compulsive love of butterflies, and all she wanted was to catch the butterfly and enjoy it for as long a time as was possible – enjoying everything about its appearance, the delicate wings, the lavish colours... she could not, the girl stressed, be content with just looking from a distance, dissolving into yearning for a favourite butterfly that was here one moment and gone the next... she wanted it to be hers and hers alone, for life, even at the expense of catching it and imprisoning it – leading to pain and distress, starvation and death.

The young woman repeated her advice to the girl, emphatic and unambiguous advice as it was: telling her that if she truly loved butterflies she should on no account continue treating them this way; once she stopped doing this, the butterflies themselves would no longer fear her and would repay love with love; they would come to her and land on her shoulders and her head, her arms and her hands – just as she pleased! The butterflies would delight in her and she in them. But the girl was unmoved: she wanted the butterflies to be with her – but as her private property, so she could touch them whenever she felt like it, for life... she could not resist this desire of hers, stronger than all else, nor did she want to resist it, as she saw nothing wrong with it... her pleasure would be impaired to the point where it could no longer be called pleasure, if she were to be separated even for a moment from the butterflies she loved... she had no choice but to continue as before, chasing butterflies and impaling them on the board and keeping them for herself... these were only butterflies after all, not (Heaven forbid) human beings...

The disguised angel looked deep into the girl's pretty face, and a sour smile parted his lips. Suddenly, without uttering another word or moving a muscle, he disappeared as if he had never been.

For a moment the girl was shocked by the sudden disappearance of the attractive young lady: she cried out in alarm, and was tempted to give some serious thought to what the other had said... but she soon recovered her composure, and her conversation with the mysterious lady and her sudden disappearance were completely forgotten, wiped from her mind.

The girl resumed her former practice – chasing butterflies, catching them in her net, impaling them alive on the broad wooden board and waiting for them to die.

One fresh morning in early spring, the girl went out to the field with her net in her hand, and suddenly her eye was caught by a beautiful butterfly perched on the golden head of a young flower, with iridescent colours such as she had never seen before. She hurried to catch it for herself, but at the very last moment, the butterfly slipped away from the net and landed on the head of another flower. The girl chased after it and the outcome was the same: the butterfly evaded the net by a miracle and fled for its life, and the process was repeated three times, five times... This rare butterfly, resplendent in its regal colours, showed remarkable agility, challenging the girl and forcing her to continue with the chase. The pursuit went on for a long time, and when the girl needed to rest a while, the handsome butterfly likewise took a break, perching on one of the luxuriant flowers of the field, and gladly imbibing its sweet nectar.

The girl took up the pursuit again and the butterfly eluded her again, refusing to be caught in the net, while the girl refused to admit defeat: she went on chasing after the strange butterfly which did not seem to know the meaning of fatigue, drawing her eyes like a magnet and eluding her grasp.

Before long the girl found herself in the heart of a dark forest, into which she had strayed unawares, driven by her irresistible impulse to hunt down the regal butterfly, the only one of its kind, and add it to her collection...

The sterile pursuit went on for some hours, until suddenly the butterfly disappeared from sight as if it had never been, and all the efforts of the girl to find it again came to nothing. The girl stood still, tired and despairing, and wept bitterly. Infuriated by her helplessness she threw away the hunting-net and flung after it everything that came to hand – branches, clods of earth and stones.

One of the stones, thrown by the girl into a dense thicket, struck a dozing tiger.

The tiger woke up, roared his mighty roar, tensed his limbs, turned this way and that and saw the girl.

The girl saw the tiger and fled for her life. The tiger was not slow setting out in pursuit of her. And when it was clear beyond any doubt that the tiger was about to catch her and rip her to shreds, the girl leapt forward without knowing what was before her, launched herself into empty space with a shriek of terror – and found herself falling to the bottom of a deep pit.

Miraculously, the girl was not badly hurt: no bones were broken, but her whole body was lacerated with deep and painful scratches.

The tiger stopped at the edge of the pit, surveyed

the scene with an angry eye, and seeing the girl lying at the bottom, trembling with fear and weeping with pain, writhing from side to side, he roared a couple of times and finally turned and went his way.

Three days and three nights the girl lay at the bottom of the pit. Her parched, bruised lips tasted neither food nor water.

On the third day she was found by a party of villagers, called out to search for her when it became clear that she had disappeared and her whereabouts were unknown.

They brought the girl up out of the pit and carried her home. The village nurse tended her devotedly and finally – she was out of danger and was herself once more.

The first thing the girl did, before even thanking her rescuers – was to rise from her sick-bed and take the board with the butterflies fastened to it with shiny metal pins; she checked to see if any of them still showed signs of life, and when she was sure there were none such, she asked to have a heavy stone attached to the board and have the board thrown into the depths of the lake close by the village.

Thereafter the girl hunted no more butterflies, not even in her imagination.

The Diamond

In the faraway days of the past, there ruled over a great people a mighty king, a sovereign noted for his valour and for his pure qualities and his wisdom. The king never went forth to war unless neighbouring peoples forced him to do so, invading his land and demanding from him and from his people territory and treasure.

During one of these wars, after a bitterly-fought battle, the majority of the enemy forces surrendered to the king's army and were taken prisoner. One of the king's generals, the commander on the battlefield, decided not to spare the prisoners but to follow the normal practice of those days and put them to death. When news of the general's intention reached the king, he did not hesitate but mounted his sturdy horse, and accompanied by a retinue of nobles and advisors he rode with all speed to the wide open space where his soldiers were busily setting up gibbets and scaffolds by the score.

The king halted his horse, observed what was going on around him, and at once sent for the celebrated general whose orders the soldiers were following. When the man stood before him, he was told to account for his actions, which he proceeded to do with a few emphatic words: these enemy soldiers had shown no mercy in combat with the king's forces, so they could expect no mercy now. The king stripped the general of his command and demoted him, and there and then he pardoned all the prisoners and set them free.

There was jubilation among the prisoners, and the king's soldiers, who had not willingly complied with their general's order, were also much relieved.

The king turned and set off to return to his court and his palace. Halfway along the road, there suddenly stood before him a shining figure not of this world, the expression on his marvellous face arousing sublime and joyful sensations in the heart.

The king stopped his horse, dismounted to approach the figure, bowed down and prostrated himself on the ground.

"Rise, O king!" – the voice of the figure rose like the sound of limpid waters: "Your deeds have been judged in the heavenly council, and you have been found worthy and a man of compassion, and it has been decided to award you a gift" – and saying this he presented to the king, still kneeling at his feet, a diamond gleaming more brightly than the skies.

"This diamond," – the figure went on to say – "will breach the wall of any besieged city, and will even win over the closed heart! Whenever you are in difficulties, not knowing what to do and where to look to for deliverance – you have only to wear this diamond on your finger and look at it – and everything hidden will be revealed to you in a flash, and the enemies of justice will disperse before you like chaff in the wind! The diamond will also heal any sickness or infirmity – in your body and in the bodies of all those whom you bless while wearing it."

The king stood rooted to the spot, and with a trembling hand took the precious stone that was offered him, and gave warm and effusive thanks for it. The figure withdrew and vanished from his field of vision. The king was left alone in the open space, holding the diamond, while his pale-faced retainers looked on in silence at him and at the gleaming jewel that had suddenly appeared in the palm of his hand, since they had neither seen the shining figure nor heard him speak.

Days passed and the diamond, set in a gold ring, a work of true craftsmanship, never left the king's finger, and whenever he spoke – he brought healing and solace to all who happened to be close by, friend and enemy alike.

And it came about that a neighbouring people invaded the land of the righteous king, and forced him to do battle. And in the course of one ferocious encounter, as he rode at the head of his armies, the king's horse stumbled and fell and threw his rider far from him, into the foaming, turbid waters of a deep river.

The king's loyal bodyguards came running and pulled the king out of the raging torrent just in time.

And when the king regained his senses, he looked anxiously at the finger where the ring should be – and there was neither ring there nor diamond. The king was saddened at heart but not dispirited: he stood up and mounted his horse, which had also recovered from the fall, and returned to the fray at the head of his armies. But this battle was unlike any other that he had ever fought – and the king was defeated, captured and sent away into exile in a land faraway. There he hungered for bread, as the ground in that place was hard, and despite all his efforts and his considerable expertise, nothing that the king planted and tended produced any viable crop.

The king's days and nights were like a stagnant stream of weariness and dejection. The king spent much of his time praying and fasting and mortifying his body. And somewhere in the recesses of his consciousness the belief began to flicker that everything that had happened to him would in the end work to his advantage; one day he would return to his land and his people.

Meanwhile the ring with the diamond, which had sunk to the bottom of the river, was retrieved by one of the enemy soldiers, who spotted it while swimming there for pleasure. And since the principal quality with which that soldier was endowed was cupidity – he ran to the nearest jeweller, offered him the ring and tried to sell it to him for an exorbitant sum. But the lustre of the diamond was so dulled that it hardly seemed to be a precious stone at all. The covetous soldier was unable to persuade the jeweller of the value of the object, and he had to be content with payment for the gold alone. But the canny jeweller could tell from the shape of the ring that the stone was a precious one, although for some reason its brightness had faded. The jeweller tried to restore the diamond's former sheen, using all the methods known to him, but to no avail. Instead of this, the stone grew even more dull than before; the treatment applied by the scoundrel-jeweller actually damaged the diamond, which no human hand had ever polished before, and he did even more harm to it than the greedy soldier had done. Finally, the diamond became the property of a slave trader, who used it as a weapon to punish his unfortunate victims, cutting strips of skin from their bodies. And the diamond became darker still, and there was no longer any ray of light which could pierce it and reach its pellucid depths, and restore to it the glory of former times.

And the exiled king, having pondered his predicament in some depth, decided that there was no point or purpose to be served by staying in this remote corner of the world, and it was not in order to live here forever, attempting to cultivate the stony ground – that he had been born into this world in the first place. After further consideration he began planning his escape in meticulous detail, a bold escape, demanding effort and ingenuity, and sure enough – his plan succeeded and he went free. The king made the long journey in all kinds of disguise until he reached his land and his people, who were glad to offer him shelter and refuge.

Tirelessly and in secret, the king organised a force of men and trained them for war. And when the time was right, he rose up against the conquerors of his land and fought them. But not all went as the king had planned it, and many of his soldiers fell. The king himself was mortally wounded and carried from the battlefield to a cottage nearby, where his physician tended him with devotion. And when for a brief moment the king opened his eyes, he saw, to his amazement, his ring of former times, lying on the sill of the window beside him. It turned out that the slave trader, in his headlong flight from the king's army, had left his instruments of torture behind in the cottage, which served as a kind of prison for those under his sway.

With his last vestige of strength, the king raised a trembling hand, took the ring, in which the diamond looked blacker than black, and put it on his finger.

The king had only to touch the diamond – blacker than black as it was, stained beyond recognition – and all the grime melted away, vanishing as if it had never been. The drab interior of that shabby cottage was bathed in brilliant light, such as had never been seen since the time that the human race first walked the earth. Not only this: the king's mortal wound healed at once, his strength returned to him and his horse, tethered outside, whinnied as if inviting him to remount and ride to the battlefield.

Without hesitation the king leapt onto his horse, and all resplendent in regal grandeur such as the eye of man never saw before, he sped to the battlefield. And his soldiers, falling back before the enemy who outnumbered them many times over, saw the king approaching and at once they drew fresh courage from a source unknown to them, and a warlike spirit set their hearts pounding, as they followed their king into the charge like a foaming torrent sweeping aside everything in its path, and inflicted a decisive defeat on the enemy.

The king's land was liberated from the invader and his people once again became free citizens, lovers of peace and haters of war, and they have remained so ever since, to this day.

And the victorious, wise and dauntless king was set to return to the capital city, to his court and his palace. And on the highway, as before, in the very same place, that envoy of the powers above again stood, shining with a lustre that not every eye could bear. And when the king dismounted from his horse and knelt at his feet with pounding heart, the envoy addressed him, saying:

"You, mighty king, wise, just and dauntless as you

are – in whom those who dwell on high delight as in their own and their only son – they meant you to have this diamond and they gave it to you, and you should know: the diamond will never shine nor impart the grace inherent in its light except when it is worn on your hand, and the purity of your heart is reflected in it. Guard it well! And you shall see, at the end of time this diamond will become an inseparable part of you – its brilliance shall be your brilliance, and your brilliance its brilliance, for ever and ever! And until then it will be a help to you in everything that you do, a cure for the infirmities of your people and your own infirmities, and it will confirm the purity of your heart, your integrity and your courage!"

The king rose from his knees, and offered his heartfelt and effusive thanks to the shining figure, who blessed him with a blessing put into his mouth by the heavenly company.

And the king guarded the diamond well, and did not take it off his hand even in the few hours of sleep that he snatched between meetings of the national council on the one hand, and the convocation of nobles on the other. And the diamond gladdened the heart of the king at all times and always, and it was the ever joyful heart of the king that gave to the diamond its life, its pure lustre and its beneficence.

The Strange
Customer

In a certain town there lived a shopkeeper, a grocer, whose boorish behaviour and crude and verbose outbursts used to drive away his customers. And although the shop was sited in a prime location, prices were reasonable and the man was honest – people still gave those premises a wide berth.

The man realised that his source of income was dwindling, and having a family to support, he declared publicly that he intended to change his ways: he regretted any offence caused to his former customers and from this day forward his attitude would be much improved; in his dealings with people, he was determined to avoid heated altercations and intemperate language.

The burghers of the town, who essentially were sympathetic towards the grocer, decided to put him to the test and they sent one of their minions to the shop, having first given him precise instructions.

The envoy entered the shop – to be greeted cordially by the proprietor, who declared himself unreservedly at his service. The customer asked for two kilograms of flour, and when this was supplied, he asked to have it tipped into a large sack that he had brought with him. Concealing his surprise, the grocer did as the customer asked and poured the flour into the coarse sack, the agreeable smile not shifting from his face.

The customer ordered two kilograms of sugar, and wanted this too poured into his egregious sack. The grocer calmed himself with the hypothesis that the man was intending to bake a cake, for which a mixture of flour and sugar was required, and he complied willingly enough, taking the packets of sugar that were stacked neatly on the shelves, and adding the contents to the flour. And after this the customer asked for a litre of oil – which was also to be poured into the sack.

The grocer's hands shook, his face contorted, the smile disappeared from his lips as if it had never been, his eyes flashed... and yet, mindful of the declaration he had made, he restrained his feelings and poured the oil into the mixture of sugar and flour.

And then came the strangest request of all: the final ingredient to be added to the mixture of sugar, flour and oil was to be – two kilograms of salt...

At this point the dam was breached: the proprietor of the shop could no longer control himself, and he kicked the sack and ejected the strange customer with curses and abuse...

And then the burghers of the town arrived and told him this was their envoy, and their sole intention had been to put him to the test, to evaluate his commitment to his solemn declaration...

The Cave

In one of the highest and most remote regions of the Himalayas, there used to exist a speedy and sure means of attaining enlightenment. In the flank of one of the sheer mountains was the aperture of a long and winding cave, and according to tradition handed down from generation to generation, the person who entered the cave, passed through it and emerged at the other end, would have enlightenment as his reward.

However, very few of those who entered the cave succeeded in traversing its full length and attaining the light. The reason being – from behind the thick walls of the cave menacing voices emerged, unearthly sounds capable of putting all aspirants to flight. Those who had made the attempt and been driven back, were for the most part deterred from repeating the experiment. The few who dared to try for a second or a third time – and they were the fewest of the few – ultimately won their heart's desire, and awoke to know themselves an inseparable part of reality.

But then something very strange happened, which at first no one could explain: among those who entered the cave there were indeed some who passed through the full length of it and emerged on reaching the other end – and they were not rewarded with enlightenment, and did not awake to see and know themselves an inseparable part of reality. The phenomenon was most unsettling, and the intellectuals among the people spared no effort in probing the issue and seeking an explanation, and in the end – the solution was found, and it was as simple and as clear as only a true and comprehensive solution can be: those intrepid people who went down into the cave, passed through its entire length and emerged from it at the other end without attaining the inner light, this in total contradiction of the accepted norms, were, quite simply and in a word – deaf. Having not been required to contend with the menace of the blood-curdling voices, they had fought no fight and were therefore unworthy of enlightenment.

So the conclusion was: the cave does not extend its favours to anyone incapable of grappling with its terrors; such a person, so long as he does not contend with these fears, is barred from attaining the light and becoming enlightened, awaking to know himself an inseparable part of reality, for ever and ever.

The Shirt of the
Happy Man

In one of the kingdoms of ancient times, there ruled a righteous king, loved by his people and respected by the kings of neighbouring lands. With the aid of his resourceful advisers and ministers, the king drafted a code of clearly formulated laws which had little to say of punishment but showed much understanding of the unpredictable nature of human beings. In a similar spirit, the enlightened king avoided frontier disputes and wars by negotiating honourable compromises acceptable to all factions. Songs were written about him; epics and ballads in all the languages spoken in those days extolled him, and he was dubbed "the king of peace and joy". Peoples, nations and their rulers, one and all, wished him comfort and contentment and especially – long life. Special prayers, appealing for such benefits on his behalf, were composed by the most venerable priests of all those lands.

But the king – like all his subjects and neighbours, those praying for his well-being and lauding his name, was only flesh and blood. And as is inevitable when flesh grows old – one day he too was waylaid by grievous illness, no respecter of persons, and he took to his bed. Pains racked him, and the joy of life which had always animated him and brought a smile to his face began to fade; as the malady persisted, it vanished from his heart altogether.

The greatest physicians of all the nations known in those days arrived in droves to attend the enlightened ruler, who seemed to be melting away in the fire of his fearful agonies – and they could do nothing. They even failed to find any way of alleviating his pain a little. Ministers, generals, advisers, priests and all the populace were at a loss as they faced the terrible blow that had befallen their benefactor.

Time passed, and hopes were running out.

One day, a stranger arrived at the gates of the palace, a man from faraway, elegantly attired but not in the style typical of the provinces of this kingdom – or of any of the neighbouring kingdoms.

It emerged that he was a physician from an unknown land, situated – according to his account – beyond high mountains and deep seas. But all these, it seemed, were no obstacle to the passage of news, telling of the righteous king and his dreadful illness. On hearing this news the foreigner had set out on the arduous journey, and after wanderings that lasted longer than a year he had arrived, with the explicit intention of trying to help the bed-ridden king.

The foreigner was admitted at once, and in the grieving hearts of the courtiers a faint ray of hope began to flicker.

The physician approached the king, put a hand on

his forehead, checked the pulse in his wrist, then stepped back from the bed and declared:

"There is a cure for the king's malady. If you can find it," he added – "he will be cured at once."

Those close to the king, his doctors, ministers, advisors, generals and companions, tensed on hearing this, and all crowded round the foreigner with staring eyes, not yet entirely purged of suspicion. The king himself, despite his pain, found the strength to sit up in his bed and gazed at the foreigner. For the first time in many months his eyes cleared, to reveal a faint gleam of hope.

"And what is the cure?" asked the senior physician of the court, in a voice both sceptical and respectful.

"The king will be cured at once," the foreigner repeated emphatically and added – "if he wears the shirt of a happy man."

"And who is a happy man?" the senior physician went on to ask, a hint of severity in his tone.

"A happy man," the foreigner explained simply, "is the man who declares himself happy."

The questioner pondered this, his head bowed. To give substance to his words, the foreigner turned to him and asked him:

"Are you happy, Sir?"

The senior physician looked up, stared into space and having considered the question at some length, replied:

"I cannot say that I am a happy man... but I am sure

that in the realm of our enlightened king such a man will be found... more than one, indeed. So we shall turn out the guard and muster the army and send men to all the four corners of the land, to seek out and find the happy man, and bring us his shirt at once!"

The king's senior general, who for decades had been required to do little, leading his army only in the ceremonial parades which marked national festivals – not that there was any shortage of these – saw fit to intervene here and he turned to the foreigner with a highly sceptical air, asking the question: "And what will happen if His Majesty puts on the shirt and is not cured?"

"He will be cured!" the foreigner insisted.

"If not, your head will be struck off in the central square of the capital!" the general threatened.

"If you will allow me!" the king interjected with a sigh, reclining again beneath the spotless bedclothes. "God did not give men heads to have them removed by the executioner! Hold your tongue, and abide by the laws of the State!"

"As Your Majesty pleases!" The broad-shouldered general clicked his heels with the jangling spurs and withdrew into the gloom of the spacious chamber, with its high ceiling and heavy curtains.

"Give instructions to your troops, and send them out in haste to search throughout the kingdom for the happy man..." the chief minister addressed the general, in a dry tone of voice.

"Wait!" – the king made an effort and sat up again on the broad bed, but as his head was spinning he had to lay it down on the huge pillow, with the royal emblem embroidered in gold. "First and foremost," he said, "you should take the test yourselves and enquire among yourselves – my dear friends and relations, my ministers and counsellors – is there not one among you who is happy?"

Those present exchanged glances and began asking one another with exquisite manners: "Is the honourable gentleman happy?" And as the questioning continued, the embarrassment increased. Finally it became clear beyond any doubt that not one among the extensive entourage of the "king of peace and joy" – was happy.

Disappointed, the king shook his head, a sign that he wanted to be left alone, and the esteemed company of ministers, relatives, friends, doctors, advisors, generals and priests – dispersed ignominiously.

Meanwhile, the troops had set out in haste to scour the land, splitting into small groups of three to save time and arrive with all possible speed at the most remote and isolated of cottages – if indeed there should be a need for this, in their quest for the happy man. It soon became clear there was indeed a need for this, since all those questioned, in all areas of that extensive kingdom which for years had experienced peace, and prosperity and affluence on a quite unprecedented scale – replied without hesitation that they were not happy. "The burden of the family is wearing me down," said the family men. "The loneliness is destroying me," said the bachelors. Soldiers were tired of peace and dreamed of wars and glory and victory, while merchants feared lest the soldiers' dreams came true, to say nothing of their habitual dissatisfaction with their profits. Priests insisted in unequivocal style that it was foolish to ask such questions, it being a well-known and established fact that happiness is the exclusive prerogative of dwellers in Heaven. Opponents of religion claimed on the other hand with equal vehemence that – soul and spirit being meaningless, all that is left is the flesh, and how can flesh possibly be happy, seeing that its future is worms and corruption, its past unrequited longings and its present – pain. Farmers complained of drought and of flood.

"I'm not happy!" was the constant refrain of all those questioned – men and women alike, without exception.

The whole kingdom was scoured and explored, down to the last dismal shack or dilapidated warehouse serving as a refuge for vagrants – and not a single happy person was discovered. One by one the envoys returned, gloomy and disappointed.

As for the king, the tension and the anticipation had intensified his pain and exacerbated his suffering, and it was decided for the time being to tell him nothing. As if the failure to find the shirt with the curative properties were not enough – it was widely feared that the results of the survey would mortally wound him and destroy him utterly. He had always considered the welfare and happiness of his realm and his subjects the central objective of his life, and his greatest achievement.

The advisors and ministers turned to neighbouring kingdoms with an urgent appeal for help, and they responded at once and sent messengers and envoys to all corners of their kingdoms, to seek out the happy man and take his shirt from him. And the disappointing results were repeated, over and over again. And when the task was completed, and all the inhabitants of those countries, near and far, had been surveyed and questioned, to the very last among them, and there was still no sign of the happy man whose shirt was destined to bring succour and a full recovery to the enlightened king – a heavy burden of grief descended upon his courtiers. "The days of the king are numbered," they concluded and added: "Alas for us that the era of wonders, of peace and prosperity such as have never been known before, at any time since the foundation of this kingdom, is drawing to a close. The golden age of our people has been cut short and will be no more!"

Then one of the advisors rose to his feet, a man of such advanced age that he had forgotten how old he was – and even his great great-grandsons, also in the king's service at that time could not say – and he mentioned a remote island, at the further end of the northern sea, beyond the boundaries of the kingdom,

"In its time," the old man began, his voice low and hoarse – "the island was the pretext for bloody wars... from time to time it was occupied by the army of one state or another... finally, when it became clear beyond any doubt that besides a few clumps of withered grass and some bare cliffs, a roost for migratory birds – there was nothing there... and even from a strategic point of view, the place had no value – the island was forgotten and abandoned... it is not even marked on the official maps of the various countries which once coveted it." This long speech clearly cost the old man considerable effort, and his hoarse voice sometimes became so choked that the speaker needed to rest for a while, to recoup his strength. His listeners watched him with some anxiety, as they had the feeling that these words of his contained a morsel of hope for the king, for themselves and for the whole kingdom, and if the old man were to pass away before completing his speech – then even this last, faint hope would be lost.

In fact, to the cautious relief of the courtiers, the old man lived long enough to conclude his remarks and to identify for them, with pinpoint accuracy, the precise location of the remote and forgotten, and formerly disputed island.

"Someone should go to that island," the old man urged. "Perhaps one of the families from days gone by is still there..."

An expedition was soon organised, and energetic soldiers rode night and day, changing horses at staging points along the way, and after ten days in the saddle they arrived at the shores of the northern sea. Exhausted as they were, they commandeered the first boat that they came upon and a day later, set foot on the soil of the rocky island.

Sure enough, clumps of grass grew here and there between the bare rocks, and a clear spring bubbled at the foot of a lofty cliff, glowing white against the pale and deep sky. Sea-birds uttered their shrill cries – and that was all.

The expedition members exchanged glances, disappointed and frustrated. For a moment it seemed to them that the whole of this frantic journey had been nothing more than a prolonged nightmare, without point or profit.

However, before leaving, the leader of the expedition, a pedantic regimental commander who was utterly committed to the objective, as he was to the completion of any mission, however futile it might be – decided to explore the base of the cliff on all sides. He did accordingly. And in one of the places where he thought he saw the outline of a path ascending, he looked up, cupped his hands around his mouth to add to the volume of his voice, and shouted with all the air in his lungs:

"Heyyyyyyyyy! Is theeeeere anyooooone up theeeeere?"

This was repeated three times, at regular intervals. And just as he was turning his broad back on the cliff, the answer reached him:

"Yeeeees!"

Astonished, he retraced his steps, looking up towards the top of the cliff. The face of a grey-bearded man, with unkempt hair, looked down at him. The expression in those bright eyes was remarkably innocent, like the expression of a child.

"Who are you?" asked the regimental commander.

"A resident of the island," was the answer.

The regimental commander wondered if there was any point in putting to this God-forsaken creature the fateful question... after all, he reasoned, the residents of the palace live in luxury and everything they ask for is presented to them on a silver tray – and they gave a negative answer. Whereas this man, up there, who has not seen a living soul in years, whose hair is uncombed and his beard untrimmed, who is buffeted by the cold winds of winter and roasted in the inescapable heat of the summer sun, who has to forage every day for food, doomed to a monotonous diet of fish eggs and crabs... how could such a wretched specimen answer the question...

The regimental commander was almost tempted to turn and go on his way. But his afore-mentioned pedantry stopped him just in time. He looked up again to the top of the cliff, cupped his mouth and directed his voice towards the old man, gazing down at him with his childlike eyes:

"Are you happy?"

"Yes!" was the clear answer, which set the heart of the regimental commander pounding. Without hesitation he cried out, in an outburst of youthful enthusiasm that surprised even him:

"Give us your shirt and you'll get a sack of gold in return!"

"I don't have a shirt," came the answer from above.

The leader of the expedition was dumbfounded. He refused to believe the man and he made haste to climb to the top of the cliff, followed by some of his minions.

When they reached the top of the cliff, an unforgettable sight was revealed to them: the endless sea kissing the far horizon and the sky descending to meet it and blending with it. A stiff breeze blew in their faces, flushed after the climb. At their feet lay the strange inhabitant of the island, a bright smile spread across his face, and he was naked as the day he was born. The pedantic regimental commander bent over him, shouted something in his ear that was meant to encourage him, and when there was no answer, he realised the man had just died, and his cry had been nothing other than a final word of farewell, on parting from this world and its creatures.

For a long time the regimental commander gazed at the cheerful smile on the face of the happy man who was no longer. Finally he stood up and began the descent of the cliff.

When the king heard the story of the happy man who had no shirt, he renounced his crown and ordered that he be taken at once to the remote island, and left there until the day of his death.

The whole of the kingdom went into deep mourning for the righteous and much-loved king, as though he were already dead. But the knowledgeable say that to this very day he is sitting on the top of the cliff, as it whitens against the infinite sky, and he is naked as the day he was born, living on a diet of crabs and fresh grass – and his limpid laughter shaking the foundations of the world.

The Cruel King

In ancient times there lived a cruel king, who oppressed his people with an iron hand, and tormented them without mercy and without restraint.

His subjects groaned under the king's oppressive rule, and when they could take no more, they rose up and rebelled against him. But their rebellions were suppressed with outstanding ferocity, foiled by the efforts of traitors and informers, who betrayed and informed to the king's agents for financial reward.

One day, there happened to arrive in that kingdom a saintly man, widely reputed as a sage and a seer of the future; nothing in the heavens above or on the earth beneath was hidden from his eyes, and whatever he said – so it would come about in the spirit and in the letter, with not so much as a jot deducted or added.

News of the arrival of the saintly man came to the ears of the king and aroused his curiosity, and the king sent a distinguished delegation of generals and rulers of the people, to greet the saint and conduct him to the palace. And the saint yielded to the persuasions of the king's generals and accepted his invitation and came to the palace, where he was greeted with much deference and lavish hospitality, as though he were a king himself.

After the banquet, with its impressive array of all

good things, the diners withdrew to one of the inner rooms in the palace, furnished with comfortable chairs and couches, and they sat at their ease about a round table, in the middle of which was a massive tray, laden with rare fruits from all corners of the world. And the king turned to the saint and asked him if he could foresee and foretell what would be his fate, and in which direction his future was tending, and what the days to come held in store for him.

The saint looked up, gazing straight into the startled eyes of the king, and he began to speak, raising his voice as he answered the question:

"Your fate, your majesty, is bitter and imminent, and disaster is dogging your footsteps and lying in wait for you, and your life hangs by a thread, a hair's breadth!" And in the same clear and fearless voice the saint proceeded to explain: "You are about to kill your brother, your father's son, blood of your blood and flesh of your flesh. And the moment your brother is murdered, the ground will open beneath your feet and swallow you alive, and you will disappear from sight, and descend in agony to the depths of Hell, straight to the blazing furnaces, and your kingdom will be divided among your generals and will fall into the hands of your enemies! But," – he cried – "if you have the good sense to act with wisdom and prevent this murder, your days will be long upon the earth, and you will know prosperity and joy, and make your kingdom strong and conquer the lands of your enemies, and when your appointed time comes, the depths of Hell will not be your final abode!" – declared the saint in conclusion.

The king was unnerved by the words of the saint, a chill took hold of him and his whole body trembled. And all the members of his entourage sat frozen in their places, their eyes fixed on the floor. Silence fell in the chamber.

The king knew his brother had been born of a different mother, and he had never seen him, since the man was a coward who kept out of sight. And the king had never shown any interest in him, as he did not envisage any danger threatening him from this quarter; the other was not likely to challenge him for the throne. On the other hand, this brother was all too likely, like any other citizen in the realm, to fall into the hands of his henchmen, who pursued suspects and rebels and people of integrity – and be murdered by them in error.

"Is it enough for me to pardon my brother, my blood and my flesh, if I am to enjoy the mercy of Heaven?" – the king addressed the saint again, to make it clear to himself and to the assembled company that he had heard and understood his words correctly.

"Preventing the murder of your brother is indeed enough to grant you every prospect of enjoying the mercy of the dwellers above, who are watching your actions with displeasure and who are aware of all your misdeeds. And there is not one of your victims whose cry does not reach their ears and is not duly recorded in their books, according to which you will be judged when the time comes."

"And how am I to recognise this brother of mine, whom I have never seen?" asked the king in a hollow voice.

"By a birthmark!" the saint declared and added: "A freckle in the shape of a crown on the shoulder, like the freckle that you have on your shoulder!"

A broad smile spread over the heavy features of the cruel king, a smile in which a significant degree of cunning malice was blended.

"If that is so," the king replied in a tone of relief, "then there is every prospect of enjoying the mercy of the dwellers in Heaven, and their full pardon!"

And the king summoned his minions and issued an edict there and then, requiring all the institutions of the kingdom and all those under his authority, to examine carefully every prisoner and every captive, any man suspected of any offence, before any harm should befall that person, and if on his shoulder a birthmark were to be found, a freckle resembling a crown – to release that man at once, unharmed, with no account taken of the alleged misdemeanour, however serious it might be. And anyone failing to comply with this instruction, to perform its requirements meticulously and to the very last detail – would suffer summary execution.

On the face of the saint appeared a broad and radiant smile of satisfaction and comfort. And he rose to his feet, bowed to the king and his retinue, left the ornate chamber and the palace, and went his way.

And all the royal institutions, the army and the police force and the royal bodyguard and the irregular units, and clerks employed in the service of the king, and spies of all kinds, hastened, in fear for their lives, to fulfil meticulously the king's command and put it into effect, in the spirit and the letter.

All the inmates of prisons and detention cells and forced labour camps, all those held in torture-dungeons, all those suspects who were yet to be arrested, anyone ever heard to utter an ambiguous word about the regime and the conduct of the king, even those already waiting beneath the gallows tree – all were hurriedly assembled in barrack squares and prison compounds, and checked and rechecked by soldiers and police officers in uniform and out, doctors employed by the crown and clerks authorised for this work. With a rough and peremptory movement, sometimes with a hand trembling out of fear or malice, or both, they pulled away the fabric covering the shoulder, exposing the living skin to view. They examined, probed, made notes which were checked and signed by witnesses. In short, they acted in full accordance with the king's explicit demand and did not deviate from it to left or right. And there was not one shoulder on which there was not found a birthmark, a freckle shaped like a crown.

The whole nation was stunned by shock and astonishment, and all were in a ferment. The soldiers and police officers, the authorised doctors, the torturers and executioners, could not believe their eyes. Finally, the investigators themselves, and the king's delegates, began exposing their own shoulders to one another and probing and checking, confirming that this symbol had alighted on their skin too, and in all the land there was not one man who could be arrested, tortured, imprisoned or hanged – as there was no man whose shoulder was clear of that royal birthmark. And the results of the inquiry and the testing were brought with due reverence to the palace and placed on the king's desk.

The king was livid with fury, but did not lose his head. He gave his generals an urgent command to go out at once and track down the saint, find where he was, confront him, and use all their eloquence in the effort to persuade him to return to the palace and present himself to the king.

The king's generals spurred on their stately horses, and at noon of that day they caught up with the saint, sitting by a stream in the shade of a branchy oak, eating his crust of bread and drinking the pure water of the stream.

And the generals dismounted from their tired horses, dirty and unkempt and their elaborate uniforms stained by the dust of the road, and they fell at the feet of the saint and prostrated themselves on the ground and pleaded with him most earnestly to return without delay to their king, who according to them was lost without him. And the saint accepted their appeal, climbed on one of the horses and rode with the generals, passing fields and forests, and as night fell he presented himself before the king, face to face.

"What is the meaning and the explanation of this?" demanded the monarch, before they had even exchanged the customary greetings. His anger was clearly visible.

"The explanation is simple and straightforward and the meaning self-evident." The saint smiled gently and added: "There is not a drawer of water in the king's court nor a hewer of wood in all the land who could not understand it!"

And the king shouted in reply, shaken to the roots of his soul:

"So all the citizens of my kingdom, the loyal and the treacherous alike, rebels and conformists too, are nothing other than – my brothers, my blood and my flesh?"

The saint confirmed this: "All of them. And if you harm a single one of them you will go down to Hell and your end will be in the blazing furnace."

"Who then is our father and progenitor?" The king's voice was still raised and his anger not yet abated, while his bemusement was growing apace.

"God, who created us so we might know the greatness of His love for us and the power of His grace."

There and then the king stripped off his finery and put on a white gown like that of the saint himself, and left the palace. There are those who say he became the pupil and devoted acolyte of that saint.

The Tiger and the Cat

It happened once, that in the depths of the dense jungle a majestic tiger encountered a wailing cat.

"Who are you?" growled the tiger, "And how dare you stand in my way?"

"I used to be a tiger," whimpered the cat in a thin voice, and added at once – "and for a whole year I've been looking for you!"

The tiger surveyed him with a look of intense, intimidating wrath. The cat trembled, and his fur bristled, but he did not turn, did not retreat or flee for his life. The tiger studied the tiny creature and realised, much to his surprise, that the other was very similar to him, could in fact have been a precise replica – albeit a pathetic one, absurdly small and utterly helpless. And despite the revulsion that the cat aroused in the regal heart of the tiger, he was also aware of the stirrings of curiosity and some faint signs of unease.

"What business have you with me?" His roar was guttural but restrained, as he did not want any of the other jungle residents to hear him talking to this dwarfish, repulsive creature, one daring to claim, with unparalleled effrontery, that he "used to be a tiger".

"I wanted to warn you, before it is too late, to behave properly and avoid transformation from the regal tiger that you are, terrible and glorious monarch of the jungle, into a blubbering cat – vulnerable and tiny and arousing scorn and revulsion – just like me!"

The words of the cat again aroused the ire of the tiger.

"Explain yourself, and be quick about it!" he roared. "And if your claim is not supported by irrefutable evidence, there is only one sentence for you – to be torn to shreds!"

"As you say, so I shall do!" The cat hastened to obey the intimidating roar of the great predator, and added in a shaky, querulous voice: "The time was, we used to go hunting together... no, not together..." the cat wailed, hurriedly amending this: "I was the one who taught you the science of ambush and the art of the hunter..."

The tiger raised a gigantic paw, and would have brought it down hard on the pitiable creature, had not the latter forestalled him by crying:

"I have proof of this, solid and unequivocal proof!" And without a pause the cat continued: "Do you remember that night towards the end of summer, when I led you to the spring under the plane trees, and told you to stay alert, because at any moment a succulent young gazelle would be coming along to slake its thirst, and you were to prey on it according to all the precepts that I had taught you so thoroughly, and demonstrated before you again and again... and when the gazelle appeared among the trees, instead of a paralysing roar, all you could utter was a contented purr... I was so angry with you, and I bellowed into your ignorant ears and even drew blood, biting your skin under the glossy young fur... And another time I taught you how to ambush a wild goat, pouncing from behind and not from the front. You messed that up too! And I had to roar at you again, lest you turn out weak and lazy, getting lost in the jungle thickets, at the mercy of the jackals. It was only at the third attempt that you got it right, pouncing on that terrified antelope..."

As the cat was speaking, recalling these events in a series of strident wails, rising and falling, the tiger abandoned his rigid stance, his muscles eased and he curled up on the ground, his eyelids drooping and his breathing heavy.

When the cat's plaintive peroration came to an end, the tiger raised his majestic head and roared suddenly:

"Who told you these stories?"

"Do you still refuse to believe," moaned the cat, a moan of pity and affronted dignity – "that I came here with one specific objective, without regard to the great danger to which I've exposed myself – to warn you against a fate as bitter as mine, since long ago I was..."

"My mother..." the tiger completed the statement with unspeakable bitterness, lowered his heavy head again, moved it closer to the cat, and cocked an attentive ear to hear what else he had to say.

"I was reincarnated in this form," the cat complained sourly and added: "Children throw stones at me, their fathers kick me without mercy, dogs chase after me and never miss the opportunity to dig their sharp teeth in me... I've got bites and bruises all over me! For a miserable mouthful of stale food I have to compete with chickens, geese, pigs, rats, ravens, and often, very often, with members of my own species. And I usually come off worse, so that permanent hunger and fear and suffering are my lot... I, who was once the mighty monarch of the jungle, with a roar that struck terror into all creatures..." the cat almost sobbed.

"Why did such a bitter fate befall you, and why were you reincarnated in this form?" asked the tiger, shaken.

"Because when I was a tiger, the mightiest tiger of them all," the cat stressed with barely concealed pride – "I didn't behave as I should have behaved."

And before the cat could carry on with the story, the tiger got in first and demanded:

"Tell me then, how am I to behave, to avoid being reincarnated as you have been reincarnated and experiencing a fate as wretched as yours?"

The cat relaxed, raised his tiny head, his eyes bright and seeming to caress his tiger son, who did not remember him and was ashamed of him and recoiled from him, and began his reply:

"Be a king worthy of the name!" And he hurried to explain: "By dealing justly, judging without favour, steadfastly seeking the good of your subjects and serving them as a living example in all your ways and deeds!"

"What does that mean?" the tiger demanded to know, his eyes narrowed in perplexity. And the cat answered him:

"You should never prey on any other creature, thin-fleshed or coarse-fleshed, for any reason whatsoever – whether it's because your anger is aroused, or you're looking for entertainment, or you need to slake your hunger."

"And how am I going to be strong and survive?" cried the tiger. "What am I to eat?" And he raised his great head, and stared at the cat with inquisitive eyes.

And the latter answered him without hesitation:

"Leaves and roots!" – and he saw fit to clarify: "There is no creature in the world that was designed to be a predator. It is laziness that has forced animals to prey upon one another. Animals prey and are preyed upon, and the end is bitter and fearful, as I explained to you just now and as you can see for yourself!" The cat pointed to himself.

"These are dreadful things that you are saying!" the tiger protested. "There is no truth in them!" he roared as if trying to ward off the words that had been said. "Anyway," he added in a softer tone, "I don't believe I could ever eat my fill if I followed your advice. I came into the world a tiger and I have the physique of a beast of prey – from my teeth and molars to my sharp and polished claws and my powerful muscles which no creature can resist!"

"So it seems to you, my dear son!" – the cat wailed, tearfully. "You have corrupted yourself and become what you have become. You have to go back to the source. Use your teeth and claws to dig up roots from the ground, and as for your prodigious strength, direct it towards the just governance of your subjects!" the cat urged.

The tiger considered what he had heard, considered it again and finally declared:

"I have no intention of changing my nature! I am a predatory tiger and so I shall remain, exulting in my might and proud of my valour!"

"And when the time comes," – the cat lowered his tiny head – "you shall become a cat, just as I am." And in a mournful tone he added: "I too was once a proud predator and I paid no heed to the advice of my mother – who was in her turn a shameless carnivore, and was transformed into a cat, drinking the full cup of disgrace and humiliation, which is the lot of the family of cats! I had no desire to hear her voice and I almost attacked her in my irritation. This voice of hers, so sad, is in my heart still!"

"I too am losing patience with your babbling!" roared the tiger, standing up. "Whoever and whatever you are, get out of my sight and be quick about it – remember that you are mortal!"

The cat fled for his life and escaped from the seething wrath of the tiger, the mighty king of the jungle.

It was not long before hunters caught up with the tiger, killed him and stripped off his hide. His proud soul was reincarnated in the form of a kitten, which rapidly grew into a cat in every respect – wailing and timid, fleeing in alarm from people and from children, from dogs and from other baneful domestic creatures.

One day the mother and the son met again – a pair of wretched street-cats, neglected and filthy and horribly emaciated, almost beyond recognition.

"How unhappy I am!" cried the younger cat, recognising the mother who had come to warn him. "If only I had listened to your voice, my fate would not have been so bitter!"

"You were arrogant, foolish and gullible, and you refused to see what lay ahead of you!" was the response.

"Come with me," wailed the younger cat in a heart-rending tone. "We should go to the jungle and try to find my three tiger-cubs, and do everything to persuade them of what the future holds for them, if they don't wake up in time."

"It will do no good, my son!" the wiser, older cat declared. "I have already been out there in the jungle, and I found my three grandchildren and warned them just as I warned you. And they were just as stubborn as I was and as you were in our time, refusing to hear and almost gobbling me up alive!"

"What will then become of the regal family of tigers?" wailed the younger cat.

"If they don't stop being predators – they will end up as cats."

Thorns

There was once an expansive land, whose inhabitants had been farmers for generations past, sowing the finest seed in the soil and gladly reaping the bountiful harvest. And it happened that one year, instead of the golden wheat that the people of this land had sown, the good barley, the superior maize and the excellent oats, their fertile ground sprouted, as far as the eye could see, a great lake of thorns and brambles.

The degrading sight, least expected of all things, struck the working men with shock and astonishment, and robbed them of speech. In spite of this, the farmers recovered their spirits, and since their granaries were still full with the produce harvested last year, they did not sound the alarm, or turn to anyone with a complaint or an appeal for help, and they did not even send a delegation to the king, enthroned in his capital city, to inform him of their predicament and ask for his advice and support; they were content with what they had, and when the time for ploughing came round again they ploughed, cleared the land of its demeaning thorns and coarse brambles, sowed the seed as in former times and prayed for rain, and sure enough the rains fell in their season and in the quantities required.

And the people of that country waited with anxious hearts, wondering how the land would repay them:

would it be as in times past, with the plains a sea of gold and ripening corn, or would that dreadful sight, which had neither peer nor precedent in the history of mankind, repeat itself – with wheat and maize replaced by a crop of thorns and brambles and all their hard work wasted, heralding a year of hunger and penury for themselves and for their families.

And the day dawned, and the time came, and the farmers made their way to the ridge of the hill from which their fields were visible, to feast their eyes on the wheat and the cereals stirring in the light breeze of dawn.

The farmers climbed up with pounding heart to that ridge and took up their positions there, standing erect and silent as in former times. And the scene was revealed before their wide-open eyes, those eyes that had yearned through so many days and sleepless nights: from horizon to horizon, as far as the eye could see, the fields yielded a tall and dense crop of thorns and brambles, moving gently in the breeze of dawn like a throng of mourners.

When the farmers recovered their wits, they turned at once to their leaders and their governors and sent them on an urgent mission to the capital city and the palace of the king, to greet him and report to him the terrible scourge that had afflicted their part of the land for two years now, to ask for advice and help and demand urgent support, lest plague and hunger kill them.

The king agreed to meet the members of the distinguished delegation, heard what they had to say and heeded their concerns. And he convened an assembly of his senior ministers and generals and summoned all those renowned for their wisdom to attend, in urgent session, to discuss the scourge, the like of which had not been known since mankind first walked upon the earth. And the illustrious ministers and the intrepid generals, the advisers and those endowed with superior intelligence, discussed the matter day and night, debating what had occurred in that part of the country, and they failed to find the merest shadow of a hint of a solution, or put forward any ideas regarding the root and the causes of the phenomenon. And since it was clear that all those regions where the thorns and brambles grew would be hungry that year, the king opened his treasury and bought stocks of grain from neighbouring countries, fortunate in that their land was as fruitful as ever, to feed his people and their cattle.

And in the third year, the inhabitants of that land once again ploughed and cleared and hoed and sowed, and with heavy heart they waited to see the fruits of their labours. And these were not slow to be revealed before their longing eyes. With the onset of spring, instead of the soft husks of the cereals, the earth once more drew up from the recesses of its subsoil those ugly-looking thorns and tall-standing brambles, which even the wind refused to stir and sport with. And a great and terrible cry went up, till the foundations of the royal palace shook, and the whole kingdom was in a ferment. And it was clear to all, that if the king's advisers, his ministers and his generals, could do nothing to halt the evil and defeat the scourge, the kingdom would be a prey to pestilence and famine, threatened by the sword of sedition at home and by foreign wars.

And the king again summoned his council, and all the men of repute and wisdom from all corners of the kingdom were invited to attend.

And they all sat down together, day and night, and raised learned proposals and various suggestions, to no avail. And because everything had been checked in the most meticulous of detail, analysed in depth and examined thoroughly, and all conclusions had been drawn, the possible and the impossible, and still the delegates to that conference did not have the remotest clue to the solution of the problem – it was decided that they must disperse, shame-faced, and publicly admit their outright failure. But before they turned to go their separate ways, one of the wisest men in the kingdom rose to his feet, a man widely renowned in neighbouring countries too, advanced in years and the scion of a distinguished family, and he turned to the king and said he had a suggestion to make – not so much advice, as a way of obtaining advice:

"I call upon His Majesty to publish far and wide,

and outside the borders of the realm as well, the announcement that the one who succeeds in finding a solution to this terrible scourge and putting a stop to it, will be appointed deputy and heir to the king, and when the time comes, will inherit his throne."

The king sighed a bitter sigh, but seeing no other course open to him, he did as that wise man suggested.

And the king's envoys set out in haste, and crossed mountains and rivers, seas and distant lands, and reported the king's promise, to appoint as his deputy and heir the man who could halt the scourge that was afflicting his kingdom.

And all kinds of strange and eccentric people made their way to the royal palace, from all nations and races, each with his own suggestion to make, but not one of these suggestions proved capable of solving the problem and averting disaster.

And the king himself and his entourage, and the people under his rule, were dejected and depressed, and there were no more amicable greetings among friends, no man whose face was not as dark as iron, not contorted by grief.

And the last of those attempting to solve the riddle and put a stop to the scourge was a man of neither style nor substance, of unfathomable age, walking barefoot and clad in rags and tatters that flapped in the wind, with long silvery beard and eyes deep, like twin pools, as limpid and as pure as mountain springs.

And the guardsmen posted at the gate of the palace

wondered if there was any purpose to be served by bothering the king with the opinions of this strange, barefooted individual who was claiming, no more and no less, to surpass in his wisdom all those men of intellect, knowledge and science, from this and from neighbouring lands, who had failed to interpret the strange phenomenon bedevilling the kingdom or to devise a remedy. But seeing that ejecting him would be a direct contravention of the king's command, to bring before him anyone who knocked on his doors and claimed he had advice to give, they opened the gate and the barefooted man entered the palace.

And the man bowed at His Majesty's feet and declared, as all the king's advisers, his ministers and generals, stood by and listened – he knew a way to put an end to the blight and halt the disaster. And as for the king's promise to appoint him deputy and sole heir, he saw no point in it; this offer he was conceding from the outset.

"Let the gentleman speak!" commanded the king, his face so lean and contorted it was barely recognisable.

And the other replied, addressing the king and his courtiers:

"Let His Majesty command all his subjects that from this day forward, they should not utter a single deceitful word – and the thorns will disappear and the brambles will be no more, and whatever you plant, that is what will grow! Sow the seeds of wheat and barley – you shall harvest wheat and barley!"

After the barefooted man had spoken there was silence in the royal council chamber with its gilded walls.

And finally, that councillor, advanced in years and of distinguished family, who had spoken up at the special conference convened by the king, rose to his feet and said:

"Since we have nothing to lose, let the king issue an edict and make clear to all his subjects that there is no alternative but to follow the advice of this stranger, and from this day forward, to have no recourse to lies, in any way whatsoever, in all senses of the word, without exception to the rule!"

And the king commanded his subjects to act in accordance with the councillor's sage advice, and his subjects, having no other option before them, hastened to adhere to the truth, not diverting from it to right or to left, and took care to avoid even the shadow of a hint of a lie – and thereafter they waited with bated breath to see what would happen and what the outcome would be.

A week had not passed since the people of that kingdom began to cleave to the truth and the truth alone, and the thorns in the fields sown with corn began to wither, and the brambles turned black and drooped, sinking to the ground, and in their place appeared the soft green husks of wheat and barley, and where the maize was planted, its stems sprang up and stood tall and proud.

And the astonished king summoned the barefooted man to his presence and thanked him in warm words drawn from the bottom of his heart, in his name and the name of his courtiers and of all his people, whom his advice had saved from the scourge of hunger. And finally he asked him, with all respect and reverence, how it was that in other countries, thorns and brambles did not grow instead of the wheat and the barley that were sown – and surely in those countries too there were liars and cheats and deceivers, no less than among his own subjects.

And the barefooted man replied:

"In your kingdom the measure was exceeded and disaster was the result. In other countries too, they are approaching the point where the measure will be exceeded and they cannot escape the scourge; they will surely die of hunger – unless they change their ways and adhere to the truth with courage and with faith, following the fine example of His Majesty's subjects!"

And the barefooted man bowed to the king and turned away, leaving the palace and disappearing as if he had never been.

The Village Girl

Many years ago, in a little fishing village, a daughter was born to poor parents. Her parents brought her up with love and faith and did everything in their power to make her life happy and to be sure she lacked for nothing. And indeed, the girl repaid her parents measure for measure, honoured them and clung to them firmly, and loved them with a pure love as they loved her.

The years passed and the fisherman's daughter grew in grace, stature and wisdom and was a magnet to all who saw her. Her smile shone with the purity of youth, like the virginal dawn of spring, her steps were light, her speech clear and pleasant, she asked pertinent questions and gave appropriate answers, and she never turned away anyone who asked for her help. The women of the village, frequently the beneficiaries of this steadfast help of hers, blessed her from the bottom of their hearts and spoke her name with joy, reverence and pride. The village girl did not tire of weaving warm woollen clothes for the old people and the children, in readiness for the harsh winters that often afflicted their village, and the old folk blessed her with tears in their eyes, and the children sang tuneful songs in her honour, mentioning her name in the same breath with the names of the most honoured and revered of the saints.

And word of the wondrous village girl took wing and spread to the neighbouring villages, towns and cities, till it reached the capital, where the king resided in his ancient palace, surrounded by eminent and self-important courtiers. The king had one son whom he dearly loved, and all the royal entourage sought ways of doing him honour, as there was no one to rival him in beauty, wisdom and noble mien.

And when the prince heard the marvellous story of this girl, living somewhere at the furthest extremity of the kingdom, on the coast, in a remote fishing-village, his heart beat fast and the desire was kindled in him to see the girl with his own eyes and hear her voice with his own ears. So the prince gave the order to saddle his warhorse, and he chose a few from the royal entourage who were reliable and wise, and rode all the way from the palace in the capital to the girl's village.

And the day the prince arrived in the maiden's faraway village, the inhabitants were celebrating the feast day of a saint who – so the story went – had blessed the fruit of the vine, and in his honour they drank goblets filled with young wine and stepped out in rhythmic dances and raised their voices in joyful song, intent on proving the truth of that most hallowed of maxims, according to which "Wine gladdens the heart of man." But the girl herself was not among the revellers, nor among the dancers or the singers. The prince found her at the bedside of a dying old lady in a ramshackle hut, speaking words of comfort in her ear, and easing her last moments with a voice sweeter than the notes of the lyre.

The moment the keen eye of the prince fell upon her, he knew for sure that he loved her, and no one could resist this love of his, stronger than death, or do anything to impair it.

There and then the young prince decided the village girl, she and no other, would be his wife and in the fullness of time, would reign at his side.

The maiden too, surprised by the prince and captivated by his charm and his radiant sincerity, felt her heart beating faster, and knew that without this youth her world would be a darker place and her life would no longer be life; she was ready to be the meanest of his maidservants if only she could be in his presence and serve him with joy and humility until the end of all generations.

They became acquainted, and the prince expressed his feelings to her, and laid out before her his intentions and his aspirations, and she listened to him with delight and accepted all that was offered her. And so it was agreed, that the prince would return to his palace, and immediately send her a distinguished delegation of nobles and grandees, to bring her with all appropriate pomp and regal ceremony to the capital city and the royal palace, where the nuptials would be celebrated according to hallowed precept and ancient ritual and the village girl would become the wife of the prince.

Not many months passed before the royal delegation arrived in the village, and the girl climbed into the carriage, harnessed to six horses white as snow and decked in gold and silver, rubies and precious stones – and all the people of the village, old and young alike, came out to see them on their way, some taking their leave of the maiden with joy and others weeping for her. Those who wept were saddened by the knowledge that they would never again look upon her wondrous beauty, and her pure and enchanting voice would ring no longer in their ears. The others shared in the happiness of the future princess and were proud of her, wishing her well and hoping she would enjoy the good fortune that she deserved more than any other.

The people of the village accompanied their favourite daughter an appreciable distance, and then the delegation halted and the last blessings were spoken. Then the royal coachman urged on his mighty horses and they, as if sprouting wings, leapt up from the rocky ground and set out at a headlong pace. And the villagers waved hands and were answered with waves of the hand, until the carriage disappeared around a bend in the road.

The royal procession passed by fields and mountains, woods, rivers and lakes, villages, towns and cities. And their residents came out to the high roads to greet with cries of joy, waving handkerchiefs and throwing hats in the air, the illustrious horsemen and the maiden sitting in her gilded carriage, harnessed to six powerful stallions.

And in the dense forest, not far from the capital city, the courtiers and the girl were confronted by the inhabitants of that place, and they were ugly of face and stunted of build, dressed in foul-smelling rags. And the forest-dwellers ran alongside the carriage, which had to slow down on the narrow and twisting path, waving filthy hands and singing their songs and dancing their dances, calling upon the future princess to deign to look into their faces, see their abject suffering and take pity on them, and do something for them, for the improvement of their lives.

The girl turned to the leader of her escort, a reasonable man, a minister and a peer, whose conduct was impeccable and courage undaunted, and asked if it were permissible to throw a few coins among the rag-wearers running alongside the carriage.

"My lady!" replied the leader of the escort. "My prince's command is to obey your will whatever it may be, and follow your instructions. All that my lady commands," the minister concluded – "shall be done!"

So the girl ordered the scattering of gold coins among the ugly forest-dwellers, the folk with the strange gleam in their oily eyes – sometimes repellent, sometimes intimidating, sometimes pitiable.

The hordes of dancers swarmed around the

carriage, snatching the coins as they were still in the air, pushing and jostling one another and trampling on the bodies of the fallen, testing with their crooked and blackened teeth to be sure the coins were pure gold and stuffing them hurriedly into their pockets, but instead of leaving the carriage alone, they crowded around it, with the result that the horses were alarmed and the coachman had difficulty calming them. And they called to the maiden, the village girl, in a loud voice, telling her that her treatment of them was cold and unfriendly, arrogant and hypocritical, and she was trying to fob them off with a handful of coins and be rid of them, instead of coming down from the carriage and proving, before all the crowd, she was not ashamed to be in their company nor was she the kind to discriminate, her feelings were sincere and she was not repelled by their abject condition or averse to their proximity, and she was ready to stay with them for a while and even take part in their dances and share in their festivities...

The girl's compassionate heart was moved for the forest-dwellers – barefoot, neglected and ugly as they were – and she ordered the driver to stop the carriage and she stepped down from it and mingled with the multitude of the dirty and the wretched, and asked how they were faring and answered their questions, and won them over with warm words and a broad and radiant smile that was all innocence and friendship. And when the strident wail of the pipes was heard, the girl was not repelled by the stench all around and she accepted the invitation to dance, and danced with everyone who asked her. And the dancing grew ever more riotous and more frenetic and the maiden, who was not accustomed to dancing and was certainly not familiar with a style of dancing such as this, felt her mind reeling, and without understanding how, she found herself in the very heart of the circle of dancers, who suddenly changed their tune and started abusing her and pelting her with lumps of viscous and stinking mud.

Accompanied by two of his officers, the leader of the escort cleared a way for himself through to the heart of the circle, and stood before the girl, whose clothes were covered in mud and face smeared with it, saluted and asked, in a tone of due deference, if it was her wish to order the dispersal of this riff-raff that was causing her grief.

"No!" the girl declared and added: "I've enjoyed their company, and the mud I can wash away in the stream over there."

And true to her word, she approached the stream and rinsed the mud from her face and from the fine garments that the prince had sent for her, no longer as lustrous and bright as when she had put them on. And the forest-dwellers disappeared as if they had never existed.

The girl climbed into the carriage and ordered the coachman to drive on.

A day passed, and in the evening the forest-dwellers appeared again in their hordes, running alongside the carriage, abusing the one sitting inside it and throwing clods of mud at her through the open window. And the leader of the escort again asked the girl for permission to disperse the rabble and the girl rejected the suggestion firmly, pointing out to him that the misery of these creatures and their wretched state had driven them out of their senses; degrading poverty and ignorance were the root causes of their loutish behaviour – and the best course would be to carry on with the journey and pay them no further heed. But at that very moment, the strident sound of the pipes was heard, and the revelry resumed, and someone stretched out a hand and opened the ornate door of the carriage, and before she knew what was happening the girl found herself in the centre of the circle, jumping and leaping to the raucous music of the ugly forest-dwellers. And when night fell, the girl was covered in thick and stinking mud, which was not easily removed from her face and her increasingly shabby formal attire. And the escorting troops looked on in silence, waiting for their young mistress to speak out; these were hardened soldiers, schooled in war and educated in combat, strong in body and resolute in mind, and they could have dispersed that rabble in an instant if ordered to do so. But the girl did not give the order, did not turn to them or say a word to them, and they sat in their saddles, watching the proceedings with stony faces.

And so the lengthy journey continued, until one evening the girl did not return to the carriage but stayed with the forest-dwellers, the fine clothes on her body turning into filthy, vile-smelling rags, her back growing hunched, the innocent and happy light no longer shining in her eyes and the radiance gone from her face which had turned dark and brooding. It seems, from that moment onward, the girl could no longer say in which direction she was heading, and when the leader of the escort tried to remind her of the prince waiting for her in his father's palace, the girl contradicted him, insisting that such things were only fantasies born out of fairy-tales, vanity of vanities and pointless delusion. If ever a prince had appeared to her, it was in a dream... And life, real life, was here, in the dense forest among its reeking denizens, and there was no escaping from them, hideously ugly as they were and ineffably, pointlessly malicious.

In spite of this the leader of the escort, the wise and steadfast minister, presented himself before the girl every morning and every evening without fail, to ask her again what she wanted and had her aspirations changed in any way, and to remind her that at her command it was within his power to disperse this distasteful rabble at once. And he also raised with her the subject of her betrothed waiting for her in his palace. But this reminder roused the fury of the girl, worn out as she was and tormented beyond recognition.

"Where is he?" she would exclaim in her bitter despair. "Is it too much trouble for him, to come and rescue me from this mess?"

"He's in front of you now," the leader of the escort used to assure her patiently, explaining: "I am his representative! One word from you will suffice, and all of this rabble will be swept away like dust in the street and dispersed to all the darkest corners of the wood, as if it had never existed!"

"And what will be left?" the girl persisted morosely, expecting no reply from her interlocutor and concluding: "Nothing! Vanity and delusion..."

And this episode has been repeating itself ever since then and even into the present day: the royal procession waits for the girl to come to her senses, stand up straight and tell the senior minister, the intrepid commander of her escort, to clear the rabble from her path and scatter them in all directions – whereupon she will climb aboard her carriage and the six stallions will bear her like a storm wind to the palace, where her heart's chosen one is waiting for her, the prince, whose love for her will never fade.

The Hump

A boy and a girl were friends, and their friendship was firm and steadfast and flawless, and they were truly loyal to each other. Everything they had they shared between them equally, and they told each other all the stories that they knew, revealed to each other all the secrets they had heard; they shared all the ideas that occurred to them and all the dreams that they dreamed, and everything that they longed for. Naturally, they also defended each other from the bullies and the street urchins who made fun of them and gave them a hard time, attacking and assaulting them on a regular basis.

In fact, it was the boy who used to fight valiantly in defence of his friend, who was unable to take part in the brawling and defend either herself or her friend, because of the large hump that deformed her back and bowed her over in a most ungainly fashion. The hump was the primary cause of the scuffles and confrontations with the street gangs; the children, in typical fashion, used to call the girl with the hump humiliating and derogatory names such as "two-legged camel", or "hump-backed mule". The boy would retort in kind, and before long the exchange of insults would turn into an exchange of blows, which usually ended with the boy lying prone in the muddy gutter, recipient of a respectable quota of punches, kicks and bites.

One day, the boy and the girl were sitting on the pavement, after a "battle" that had left fresh bruises on their faces and bodies, and the girl turned to the boy, who was doing everything he could to cheer her up, and told him that she was sick of her life as it was, and it was absolutely clear to her that she had nothing to look forward to but bitter disappointment, pain and searing, infuriating insults, and her heart told her that the best option for her was to put an end to the poisonous derision, and the interminable suffering of body and of mind...

In vain the boy tried to persuade her otherwise, and prove to her, citing all kinds of conclusive evidence, that all this would pass and they would grow up and no longer be easy prey for the street children; he added that there were eminent people who were also hunchbacks, and finally he said he would never, ever, abandon her, until the end of all time. With all the eloquence that he could muster he begged her and entreated her to take pity on him and not leave him all alone in a world of such meanness and cruelty... But the girl refused to listen, and she left her loyal friend and returned to her own home, determined to put an end to her miserable existence.

In his bitter despair, the boy fell to his knees in the place where his friend had left him, and with tears in his eyes and arms outstretched, he cried out to the heavens and demanded that justice be done and asked that He, the one renowned for His boundless mercy, show mercy to his unhappy friend. And even before the cry fell silent, a shining figure appeared before the boy, as he still knelt – a vision of majesty and splendour, smiling serenely and saying:

"The world is founded on the justice and the mercy that you asked for, and on them it depends for its existence."

"Then remove the hump from my friend's back!" cried the boy, recovering from his surprise.

"If the hump is removed – it will not be mercy, nor will justice be served!" was the distinct answer.

"I don't understand this!" protested the boy who had prayed.

"The way you comprehend is such that you cannot understand. But if it is your earnest desire to discover the reality of justice and know the quality of mercy – then you must experience them at first-hand."

"And how do I do this?" the boy demanded impatiently.

"By taking on the hump of your friend, if she agrees, for one whole day and carrying it your back," the radiant figure declared. "Are you ready to do this?"

"Ready and willing!" cried the boy joyfully, rising to his feet.

"Do it then!" the figure commanded, and disappeared from his sight.

The boy went in search of his friend and found her

in the corner of a dank cellar.

"Tell me you are ready and willing to have your hump transferred to my back, and it shall be done! Say it! Speak!" exclaimed her courageous friend.

And before she realised what she was saying, a cry emerged from the girl's lips, and she agreed.

At that very moment she felt a huge sense of relief, as if a huge stone had been removed from her back. Her body, bowed down for as long as she could remember, was suddenly straightened – whether she wanted it so or not. Impulsively, she put her hands behind her back and with trembling fingers tried to feel the hump – but no trace of it remained.

Without saying a word, the girl ran outside, like a bird suddenly released from its cage and heeding the call of freedom, while her friend, bent double and struggling under the weight of the great hump, hobbled ponderously behind her.

With considerable and unaccustomed effort, he managed to catch up with his friend; he was so delighted by her happiness, he almost wept. He wheezed and panted, his heart pounding with joy and exhilaration – and from the exertion of carrying the weight. Meanwhile the two of them were seen by a group of children of their own age. For a long moment the onlookers stared at them as if rooted to the spot, mouths gaping and eyes open wide, refusing to believe what they were seeing: a mischievous girl, all aglow with joyful charm, as light as a feather, prancing on the cobblestones – and trailing along behind her, a boy bent down almost to the ground under the weight of a massive hump, breathing heavily in a desperate attempt to follow his friend's example, his clumsy gait eliciting only peals of laughter.

The girl stopped and stood still, turned and saw her loyal friend carrying her hump on his back. His eyes awash with joyful tears, he caught up with her, and held out a warm and trembling hand to her as he had done so many times before. The girl said to him:

"I won't touch your hand lest the hump come back and attach itself to my back again. Can you forgive me for this?"

"Of course!" cried the boy warmly. "From now on, we don't have to hold hands anymore! Let's carry on with the game that we started this morning, before those idiots interrupted us, as they usually do!"

"I'm afraid there's no point in finishing off the game we started this morning," the girl replied calmly, with a charming smile. "I am so much faster than you are, and you can't be my partner in the game anymore!" And saying this, she turned to a gang of surly ruffians and called out to them: "Anyone who wants to play with me, come now! I am sure I can beat all of you easily, at any game you choose!"

The children recovered from the shock and suddenly burst into loud and ringing laughter, resonant and harmonious to the ear, the wholesome laughter of schoolchildren. And then, as if a signal had been given, the laughing children fell upon the boy with the hump, just as they had attacked the girl on a number of occasions. The boy was knocked to the filthy ground, the recipient of punches, bites and kicks... Were it not for a workman who happened to be passing and dispersed the urchins, the boy's fate would have been unenviable indeed.

"You don't have many friends round here, do you?" asked the workman sympathetically, in a tone blending compassion with a sizeable hint of distaste.

"I do!" the boy replied, clearing his throat and standing unsteadily, spitting blood. He turned this way and that, but could see no one.

The boy returned to his home, but his parents did not recognise him and at first refused to believe his story. It took some time to convince them. And when they were finally persuaded beyond a shadow of a doubt that this ugly, deformed creature with the huge lump on his back was indeed their son, the parents fell into each other's arms, and wept long and bitterly over the malign fate that had dealt them this cruel and merciless blow.

The boy sat in his little room, and deep in his heart he hoped his friend would come, to ask after him, comfort him and apologise for her behaviour – the result no doubt of her relief and exhilaration following liberation from the burden of the hump. But she did not come.

Late at night, the boy slipped out of his parents'

home, arrived at his friend's house, and as had always been his custom, tried to wake her by throwing handfuls of sand at her window.

The girl opened the window and leaned out over its broad sill. The boy once more expressed his delight at knowing she was finally rid of that fearful hump. Only now did he realise how heavy it had been, and what immeasurable suffering it brought to the one who bore it. Surely, the boy added – since his friend did not react or respond to his words, and he felt awkward, not wanting the conversation to end so abruptly – surely the distress that had afflicted her before had passed never to return, and she saw how truly wonderful life could be, and there was no reason to loathe it, and his joy was her joy and he hoped to see her the next day at their usual place, which she knew so well...

"If indeed my joy is your joy," the girl replied finally, in an unfamiliar voice, pleasantly modulated and assured – "don't bother going to our usual place, or anywhere else for that matter. The sight of your hump is painful to me and it brings back unpleasant memories, and above all, it arouses in me feelings of revulsion which I cannot resist... You know I have always been honest with you and now I am telling you plainly – I can't spend time with someone who has a hump or be his friend, not ever!"

And the boy answered in a shaking voice that he understood her feelings and would no longer trouble her with his presence, or expect her to look at that hideous hump, and his only hope was that the happiness she had gained after such long suffering, and the joy of which none could be more deserving, would continue unimpaired until the very end of time.

The girl heard the words of her long-time friend, stepped back and silently closed the window. And the boy returned to his home, weeping bitterly all the way, and the tears continued to flow when he took to his bed, the great hump vibrating to the rhythm of his sobs.

The next day at the appointed time, the hump disappeared from the back of the boy and attached itself once more to the girl, bending her proud back.

And the shining figure appeared again before the boy:

"Are your eyes now open to see and your heart to understand?"

"No!" exclaimed the boy, "I shall never understand! I don't want my friend to suffer, no matter how selfish she has been, how unspeakably cruel. Her happiness is my happiness, and her joy is my joy!"

And the shining figure replied:

"There can be no happiness so long as selfishness rules the heart, and cruelty – is its expression! The hump on your friend's back will teach her to rid herself of selfishness and cleanse herself from cruelty – and thus she will gain happiness. You must help her in this, you must make her understand the purpose of the hump in her life and tell her that the moment she purges the selfishness from her heart and renounces cruelty – the hump will disappear from her back, never to return!"

But the boy refused to be comforted and would not accept the reassurances of the divine envoy. The latter thought for a while, before finally looking up and addressing the boy again:

"Go to your friend and ask her consent to have the hump transferred back to you for whatever period of time you agree on: if a day – then a day, if a month – then a month, if a year – then a year, if forever – then forever."

The heavenly messenger disappeared, and the boy ran to his friend. He found her in the depths of bitter despair, beset by intolerable anguish. Before she could speak, he called to her:

"I have the promise of the heavens that I can again carry your hump on my back for whatever period of time we agree on between us: if a day – then a day, if a month – then a month, if a year – then a year, and if forever – then forever. For my part, I implore you to agree that the hump be moved to me forever! As your happiness is my happiness, and your joy is my joy!"

And the girl with the hump looked up at her long-time friend, gazed tearfully into his eyes – radiant with ineffable purity – and declared:

"I will not allow you to carry my hump for even one minute! From this day forward I will bear it on my back with joy, for I have learned from you what love is."

And even while the girl was still speaking, the hump melted away from her back and vanished, as if it had never existed. And the two children froze for a long moment, stunned and bemused by the wonder that had befallen them, and when they recovered their wits, they fell into each other's arms in a long and firm embrace. And when they separated, they knelt down and gave thanks from the depths of their purified hearts for the justice and the mercy that God grants to all.

The Dragon down the Amazon

It was the ambition of a young and enthusiastic priest to bring the gospel of salvation to the primitive tribes dispersed along the lower reaches of the Amazon. He asked after, and found, a certain tribesman, advanced in years, who had settled in one of the new townships which were proliferating at the time as a part of the Brazilian development programme. He befriended him, and in exchange for a dozen bananas per day, and a handful of tobacco leaves, of the local variety, he learned something of the native dialects spoken in those places. After a prolonged fast, to prepare himself from both a spiritual and physical viewpoint for completion of the task before him, the man boarded a canoe and set off on his voyage down-river. The equipment that he took with him comprised: a tattered Bible with a binding of antique vellum, the clothes that he wore and an unshakeable faith in God, which filled his heart to overflowing.

It was not long before the pious young man noticed a number of tribesmen, hiding among the dense shrubs on the bank of the river and watching him keenly. Without fear or trepidation, he paddled his canoe to the shore, raising his hand in greeting and smiling broadly – and addressed them in their own language.

The members of the tribe were stunned, hearing

the words of greeting so familiar to them, emerging from the mouth of a stranger. They left their hiding-places and rather awkwardly, still looking at him with suspicion, stood facing him, their weapons ready to hand. He asked them, again in their own language, which sounded most agreeable to their ears, to take him to their village, and they complied with his request, not demanding to know the reasons behind it.

The young priest enjoyed a friendly reception among the natives. They even allocated him some living-space, in the corner of a spacious straw hut belonging to one of the most distinguished families. He did not spend his time idly, but began at once preparing the ground for the accomplishment of his sacred mission.

Patiently he listened to the natives' stories of the spirits controlling the lives of men and of beasts, and politely he presented his own perceptions, backed up by instructive parables which spoke to the hearts of his hosts. He also listened every evening, attentively and without protest, to the interminable perorations of the tribal wizard, who was in the habit of preaching while wearing the intimidating mask of a predatory animal. At first, the latter used to expel him from his congregation, evidently seeing him as an unwelcome competitor. But in the end the guest succeeded in befriending him, whereupon he was not only admitted to the congregation, but was told he was considered a member of the tribe. On one occasion, the wizard delivered a sermon of greater than usual length, in the course of which he revealed the startling secret of the tribal dragon, enthroned in splendour on a hill surrounded by trees and bushes, to whom sacrifices were offered, sometimes animal and sometimes human.

In fact, the secret was a secret only to the guest. And it was revealed to him with the intention of proving to him explicitly the degree of trust that the tribe and its wizard placed in him.

The young man rose at once and asked permission to see the dragon at close quarters.

After much hesitation, and secret confabulation between the elders of the tribe and the wizard, it was decided to accede to the request of the visitor – in view of his newly acquired status as a resident with equal rights and obligations – to see, if only from a distance, the lair of the fearful dragon and, if he were lucky, to catch a glimpse of the monster itself.

The day after these discussions, the procession set out – its destination, the hill-top abode of the dragon, the suzerain of all the neighbourhood.

At the head of the procession strode the tribal wizard in his scary mask, to his right – his eldest son, and to his left – the new guest of honour, none other than the young priest. Behind them, all the members of the tribe walked in silence.

When the procession reached the foot of the hill, a signal was given by the tribal wizard, and the womenfolk of the tribe, and their children, came to a halt. The men went on, climbing the hill and advancing another hundred metres or so. The signal was repeated, and the men too stopped where they were and went no further. Only the trio – the tribal wizard, his eldest son and the young priest – went on in silence towards the top of the hill. As they approached, the tribal wizard pointed to a tall bush, with dense foliage, and the three of them moved in that direction.

With immense caution, the tribal wizard bent the flexible twigs of the bush, parting them with his hands and signalling to the priest to approach and look through the little peephole thus created towards the top of the hill. The latter needed no second invitation. He approached the wizard, and over his broad shoulder peered in the direction indicated. On the top of the hill, beneath the shade of a low and broad-leafed tree, there appeared before his eyes, in all its pomp and majesty – the bloated shape of a giant pumpkin.

"Is that really the fearful dragon?" he whispered, gesturing towards the miraculous pumpkin. The wizard moved quickly to protect him, putting the twigs back in their former place and closing the peephole, while quietly chiding the priest for the risk he had taken upon himself – speaking in the vicinity of the monster and thereby endangering not only himself but also the whole tribe, which could yet be the target for vengeful action on the part of the dragon whose honour had been impugned. The young priest sensed the terror behind the grotesque mask of the wizard; the exposed half of his body was drenched in sweat. Finally the wizard confirmed that yes, this was indeed the monster, in all its awful grandeur.

The young priest burst into loud peals of laughter, and before his companions could recover their wits, he was running towards the monster, paying no heed to their frantic warnings.

When he stood before the huge pumpkin, he turned and saw all the members of the tribe advancing cautiously, gathering among the bushes and watching him tensely.

The young priest took a penknife from his pocket and cut into the thick flesh of the prodigious pumpkin. Then he turned to gauge the reaction to his deed among the crowd of onlookers, but even before he turned he found himself pelted with a hail of stones and clods of earth, some falling around him, the better-aimed hitting him. He heard panic-stricken cries, ordering him to leave the holy site at once. His death-sentence was proclaimed there and then – although at a distance, since the natives were afraid to move any closer to the sacred dragon, whose prestige he had dared to defile.

The young priest was left with no choice. Shaken to the roots of his soul by this unexpected reaction, he fled for his life.

The time he had spent among the natives had helped to give him some familiarity with the terrain.

All the same, it was no easy task to evade his pursuers and escape from the stones that were still raining down on him, and later – from their whistling arrows, tipped with poison.

He hid in a deep hole near the river, while the angry cries of the hunters and the thunder of their feet rang in his ears and struck terror into his heart.

The hole was narrow and allowed for no movement at all; if he were to attract the attention of those intent on killing him, he would have no escape. Various insects sensed the foreign body that had invaded their dark domain, and made every effort to be rid of him, voraciously biting his tender and unprotected flesh. The priest covered his mouth with both hands, afraid of uttering a sudden cry of distress. He could clearly feel the bitten parts swelling up there and then, accompanied by searing pain which drove him to distraction and made him begin to doubt his own sanity and even his own identity.

In the dead of night, when the neighbourhood no longer reverberated to the shouting of men and the drumming of bare feet, the fugitive climbed out of his hole and made his way, slowly and painfully, to the bank of the wide river. Before long he found an abandoned canoe – the same one in which he had arrived a few months before, when his heart was filled with divine, all-conquering enthusiasm, and the achievement of his goal seemed to be in the palm of his hand.

The enthusiastic young priest returned the same way he had come. But he did not admit defeat. Three years later, in different clothing and with a somewhat changed appearance, he returned to those shores and was received as he had been the first time. He played on the linguistic sensibilities of the natives, as a means of bringing enlightenment to their souls, and finally, when he had befriended them sufficiently and earned their trust, he was introduced to the secret of the existence of the tribal "dragon".

Now as before he asked permission to feast his eyes on it, and after the familiar rituals, he stood in the company of the tribal wizard and his son behind the dense bush, peering through the foliage at the pumpkin, which seemed to have grown in size and in weight. This time, learning from the experience of the past, he did not run to plunge his penknife into it, but he approached it with awe and reverence, put out his hand and caressed the thick skin, and even appeared to be conversing with the creature – much to the relief of the natives, who were standing by and nervously watching proceedings.

Days passed and on the day of the tribal festival, once again the guest went to visit the "dragon", and this time he stood erect before it, without any of the reverence that he had shown on the previous occasion. The "dragon" made no apparent response to this, and it was assumed that the creature had taken no offence.

A few days later, when the prevailing opinion was that the young priest was the chosen friend and confidant of the "dragon", they all plucked up their courage and approached the dragon under the guidance of the guest, the tribal wizard and his son. Those two had also laid hands on the rough hide of the pumpkin and it seemed, without a word said, they too had been accepted into the circle of the monster's friends.

When finally, all the members of the tribe, men and women, young and old, had climbed to the top of the hill and put their trembling hands on the scaly skin of the "dragon", and the latter had not responded, and nothing had happened – they were overwhelmed by a great, ringing outburst of relieved laughter, which rolled on and on, raising echoes far and wide.

With united effort the natives began moving the "dragon" from its place – and still the fearsome teeth were not bared.

It was time for the guest to explain calmly, in the dialect they understood best, precisely what a pumpkin is and what it is used for.

A great tribal banquet finally obliterated all traces of the former "dragon". The natives stopped inventing monsters for themselves and paid more attention to the words of the young priest, whose prestige now soared to the heavens; in the meantime he had grown older, and had learned to wait patiently for the right moment to bring the truth of God before His creatures.

The Rabbi and his Neighbour

In one of the Jewish townships of Eastern Europe, in the days when they still existed, and sometimes were even prosperous, living side by side were the wealthiest man in the township and a poor rabbi.

The spacious house of the wealthy man, with its two lofty storeys, overlooked the rented house of the rabbi, which had formerly served as a wood-store. The rabbi, widowed not long before, had young children to support, and his home was derelict: the door hung on one hinge, the single window was broken, and the backyard, little more than a narrow passage, had reverted to the function of the former storehouse and was crammed with piles of wooden planks.

Every morning the two men, the wealthy burgher and the poor rabbi, used to stand at their windows and pray. The rabbi, praying in a full and melodious voice, used to conclude with the brief statement: "I thank you, God, for supplying all my needs." The wealthy man, his devotions not yet finished, would rise upright from his prayerful pose on hearing this declaration, looking long and hard at the broken window of the rabbi, his neighbour, before returning to his prayer-book. The rabbi, who sometimes did not have so much as a crust of coarse, salted bread to eat, adhered to this bizarre practice and never stopped thanking his God, every morning, for "supplying all his needs".

This constantly repeated phrase began to grate on the wealthy man's ears, and since he found it was distracting him from the proper observance of his own obligations, it aroused his anger too. One fine morning, the wealthy man could restrain himself no longer, and hearing his neighbour repeat those words yet again, he slammed shut his prayer-book – trimmed in silver and studded with precious stones – threw it down on the table and hurried to the rabbi's house. He passed through the gate of the yard, and breathing hard, partly from haste and partly from the fury that consumed him, he stood by the broken window of his poor neighbour. The latter was busy folding his moth-eaten shawl and laying it on the broad shelf beside him.

"With respect, Sir!" cried the wealthy man forcefully – "I am minded to ask you a question," – and without waiting for the rabbi's response he went on in a bemused and angry tone of voice: "What do you mean by giving thanks every morning to the Holy One Blessed be He for 'supplying all your needs'?" And he went on to add by way of explanation: "Are you giving thanks for your abject poverty? For your derelict house? For your widowhood, and your inability to afford so much as a crust of coarse bread to sustain you? For the children you must support? Are these your needs?" the wealthy man fumed.

"Apparently so," the rabbi answered him calmly and withdrew into the radiant gloom of his house.

Mathematical Epilogue (don't panic!)

Pythagoras asserts that the number nine (9) is the symbol of love (AMOR – "A"). If we pursue this line of thought, we shall find that the obstacle to the revelation of love in every individual (INDIVIDUAL – "I") is egoism (EGO – "E").

It is a mathematical fact that any whole number, minus the sum of its digits, equals a number fully divisible by nine, the sum of its own digits also being a multiple of nine.

Take any random whole number, for example: 12243; 1+2+2+4+3 = 12; 12243-12 = 12231, a number that is fully divisible by nine, with digits equalling a multiple of nine.

Where the whole number symbolises the Individual (I), and the sum of digits symbolises Egoism (E) – you need only to take the egoism from the individual to be left with the revelation of love. Thus: I-E = A.

Like all of us, the protagonists of these stories carry love (Amor – A) within themselves; some of them manifest it and act in accordance with it, by dispelling the Ego (E) from their individual selves (I).

Shlomo Kalo's other short fiction collections:

The King Whose Name is Love, published in Israel, Spain, India, Brazil, the Philippines and Korea. Available on www.y-dat.com, www.y-dat.co.il, and on Amazon.com starting 2017.
The Dollar and the Gun, published in Israel, The UK, Italy, India, Greece, Romania, and Serbia. Available on www.y-dat.com, www.y-dat.co.il and on Amazon.com starting 2017.
Forevermore, published in Israel and in Romania. Available on www.y-dat.com, www.y-dat.co.il, and on Amazon.com.
Kidnap, published in Israel.

Novels and fiction titles available in English:

The Chosen, published also in Korea and in Israel. Available on Amazon.com, www.y-dat.com and on www.y-dat.co.il.
Lili, published also in Israel Available on Amazon.com, www.y-dat.com and on www.y-dat.co.il.
Athar, published also in Israel Available on Amazon.com, www.y-dat.com and on www.y-dat.co.il.
Erral, published in Israel. Available on www.y-dat.com, www.y-dat.co.il and on Amazon.com starting 2017.
The Self as Fighter, published in Israel, the UK, Spain and Bulgaria.

Author's biography

Nominee for the Nobel Prize in literature, Shlomo Kalo, was born in 1928, in Sofia, Bulgaria. From the age of 12, was active in an anti-Fascist underground. At the age of 15, was arrested and exiled to a concentration camp. At the age of 18, won a prize in a poetry competition. Studied medicine in Prague where he also worked as a journalist. As an overseas volunteer for the newly established Israel he was sent to train as a pilot in Olomouc. Immigrated to Israel in 1949. Was awarded M.Sc. in microbiology by the Tel-Aviv Univ. Became director of medical laboratories in Israel's largest health care service.

The sharp turn in his life which occurred in the first week of 1969 has been reflected ever since in his creation. About 80 books of his were published in Israel: literary fiction and literary non-fiction on a variety of contemporary, spiritual, philosophical and scientific themes. Some of Kalo's works have been translated and published in 16 countries. Shlomo Kalo died at his home in 2014 his last words were: "Everything is excellent to the one who is not subjugated".

www.ingramcontent.com/pod-product-compliance
Lightning Source LLC
Chambersburg PA
CBHW051645260626
47170CB00004B/1348